Secrets of a
First Daughter

Also by Cassidy Calloway:

Confessions of a First Daughter

Secrets of a First Daughter

Cassidy Calloway

HARPER TEEN
An Imprint of HarperCollins*Publishers*

HarperTeen is an imprint of HarperCollins Publishers.

Secrets of a First Daughter
Copyright © 2010 by Working Partners Limited
Series created by Working Partners Limited
All rights reserved. Printed in the United States of America.

Library of Congress Cataloging-in-Publication Data
Calloway, Cassidy.
    Secrets of a First Daughter / by Cassidy Calloway. — 1st ed.
        p.   cm.
    Summary: High school senior Morgan Abbott, the daughter of the presi-
dent of the United States, tries to hide a secret romance and stay out of trouble
on an official visit to London.
    ISBN 978-0-06-172442-8
    [1. Presidents—Family—Fiction.   2. Dating (Social customs)—Fiction.
3. London (England)—Fiction.   4. England—Fiction.]   I. Title.
PZ7.C13457Se 2010   2009049485
[Fic]—dc22   ·   CIP
                                                                     AC

Typography by Alison Klapthor
10   11   12   13   14   CG/RRDH   10 9 8 7 6 5 4 3 2 1
❖
First Edition

With love to Ken and Sophie.

Thanks for putting up with the madness.

With special thanks to Kathleen Bolton.

Chapter One

How could I have so many options but no real choice?

I scanned the pantry shelves again. "Fifteen varieties of vanilla, and not one bag of chocolate chips anywhere." Arg!

It wasn't the first time I'd wished the White House steward would let me stock the kitchen pantry in the residence wing. Who wants to eat Norwegian sardines and melba toast crackers made from organic whole wheat?

I rose to my tiptoes and reached into the deepest recesses of the pantry's top shelf. My fingers unearthed a packet of dried sour cherries. Ooh, killer. The possibilities started clicking: cherry-mocha cheesecake? Pancakes drizzled with cherry-flavored syrup? Would cherry-cheese biscuits taste delicious or disgusting? I only had one bag of cherries. Decisions, decisions . . .

The smell of smoke snapped me out of my culinary fantasies. Yikes! I'd forgotten to set the timer on the last batch of blueberry-pecan scones. Maybe I should've waited before starting on the cinnamon-chip-and-coconut muffins and the crunchy peanut butter cookies for Mom and the crew down in the Oval Office. I was stressing out, and when I stressed out, I baked. Lots.

Chill, Morgan. It's one test . . . one test that will determine the rest of your entire life!

Suddenly it was hard to breathe. I felt as if all gazillion pages of the United States government budget had been plopped on my chest. Why did my every move have to reflect on the leader of the free world? Like I needed that on top of the regular stress that comes with the SATs. Usually I could bake my way to relaxation; mixing random ingredients and walking the thin line between taste-bud explosion and gag reflex. Except this morning it wasn't working.

"Morning, Puddin' Pop." Dad sauntered into the kitchen wearing jeans and a bomber jacket, office attire at Abbott Technology, his Fortune 500 company. Mom had finally convinced him to shave off his goatee with the argument that the First Gentleman shouldn't look like a roadie at a rock concert, but she still couldn't get him to wear a business suit for anything other than official White House occasions. Not even the president of the United States could tame my father. Which made him pretty cool in my eyes.

"You're up . . . early." Dad dubiously surveyed the cookies, scones, and muffins heaped on the kitchen table. "Is this your way of getting ready for your big trip abroad?" he asked, picking up a scone and taking a huge bite.

"I can't wait to visit London." I sidestepped the question of why I was baking like a fiend. "It's my first official overseas trip where I'm not going to be stuck in a hotel room with a bunch of Secret Service while you guys have all the fun."

"Well, if you call two-hour photo ops and endless reception lines fun. I feel bad I'm not going with you and Mom this time." He paused for effect. "*Not*." Dad popped the rest of the scone into his mouth. "Hey, this is pretty good. The bottom's not even burned."

"So funny." I paused, reflecting my dad's comic timing. "*Not*."

"Speaking of London, though, you'll have to really watch yourself over there. Your mother and I have been mostly successful getting the press off your back, but now that you're growing up, they're getting more aggressive. They'll follow your every move: what you're wearing, who you're with . . . even if you're overseas."

"I know." Boy, did I know. Over the last few weeks I'd dealt with unflattering photos splashed in gossip rags, salacious rumors, and downright bad press. When you're the First Daughter, you're media roadkill. Everyone wants to dig into your life and throw it open for a quick buck.

And since screwing up was a natural talent of mine, the press had coined a new nickname for me: National Disaster.

Dad reached for another scone. "These are great. Mind if I take a dozen to the office?"

"Take two dozen. There's plenty to go around." I waved my hand over the crowded table.

Dad kissed the top of my head on his way out of the kitchen, a sack of scones in hand. A few minutes later, Mom breezed in wearing her red power suit. She took one look at the goodie-packed table and said, "What's wrong?"

"Good morning to you, too, Madam President." I made sure my expression remained bland. She couldn't know I was up to anything. This was going to be tricky—because she always seemed to sense when I was up to something. "I, uh, wanted to bake a few treats, uh, to share with the junior staffers in the West Wing."

"A *few* treats?"

"Yeah. Scone?" I handed Mom a warm blueberry-studded scone fresh from the oven.

She took it, but her sparkly brown eyes, the ones I had inherited, narrowed in suspicion. "You don't bake like this unless something's bothering you."

4

"Mom, c'mon." I gave her a gee-whiz-I'm-just-a-kid smile, the one that could be counted on to soften her up like butter. "What could be bothering me?"

Mom countered with her I'm-not-in-the-mood-to-entertain-any-b.s. expression she'd perfected over the years. Well played, Mom. Well played.

"I don't know, you tell me," she said.

The smile on my face began to wobble a little. Oh no, I was going to blow it! Luckily, the PDA in Mom's jacket pocket beeped.

"It's Humberto," she said after she'd fished it out and glanced at the screen. "The Joint Chiefs are waiting for me in the Cabinet Room."

Humberto Morales, Mom's chief of staff, my hero! "Here, take some muffins with you." I shoved a loaded plate at her. "Maybe the Joint Chiefs would like a snack while you're discussing how to save the world from terrorist threats."

"Hm, do you think this might help them take the news that I'm about to cut their budget a little easier?" Mom quipped. "I've got to run, but maybe we can talk tonight."

"Sure thing." I'd worry about how to avoid that discussion later. For now, the prime objective was to get Mom out the door before she asked any more uncomfortable questions. Like how I did on the SAT. I shut the door behind Mom and briefly leaned against it.

I bombed. There. I said it. The daughter of the president of the United States choked taking the SAT. How's that for a headline?

Okay, maybe *bombed* is too strong a word. But my scores would never secure a place at an Ivy League college. As painful as taking the SAT was, it would be even more painful to show my pitiful scores to my parents, so I'd secretly scheduled a retest today in the hopes I could raise the score to non-suckitude levels.

But right now, I had a different secret mission to attend to.

Thankful that Mom and Dad were too busy to ask their usual million questions about my day's "agenda" (like I ever planned anything out in advance), I wrapped up some warm scones, poured fresh-brewed organic Kona coffee in a thermos, and edged out of the kitchen. I'd have to be sneaky to pull this off.

At the end of the hall in front of the Secret Service's com center (a desk loaded with GPS tracking devices, monitors, and inscrutable wireless gadgetry), a tiny woman in a no-nonsense black pantsuit talked to Parker, head of my mother's security detail. At first glance, one might take her for an elf or a pixie: Short-cropped white-blond hair sprang from her skull like milkweed. I had to move fast— if she turned and caught sight of me, her enormous green eyes would swallow me up in a cauldron of suspicion and exasperation. I'd seen those tiny hands grip a government-issued sidearm and wield it with supreme assurance. I'd also seen her drop a man three times her size and put him in a headlock before he had a chance to scream. This was *not* a person to mess with.

Georgina "George" Best—my new Secret Service agent—scared the crap out of me the way no other agent on my security detail ever did. It takes epic ingenuity to give her the slip, and nine times out of ten I failed to do it. I swear it's like she implanted a GPS chip in my brain so she could track me.

I held my breath and tiptoed along the hallway wall until I reached the door leading to the back stairwell. From there it's a straight shot down to the basement. Carefully I eased the door open, keeping an eye on George.

The hinge on the door squeaked ever so slightly.

At the opposite end of the hall, George stiffened. I froze. If she caught me before I could complete my mission, I was sure I'd have a breakdown. It was super important that I sneak away. My sanity depended on it.

Luckily, Parker saved the day by offering George one of the cinnamon-chip muffins that I'd placed on the desk earlier that morning, distracting her for one second . . . and one second was all I needed.

Chapter Two

I gripped the blazing-hot thermos of coffee in one hand and a bag of scones in the other as I headed down two flights of stairs. Luckily it was Saturday, so the multitude of staffers working in the White House basement—flower shop, the curator's office, the kitchens—didn't start their weekend shifts until later. I scooted down the basement hallway, deftly avoiding housekeeping carts, stacks of hotel pans, and a forgotten delivery of kale left out of the cold storage room. My destination: the carpenter's shop.

Hey, it wasn't glamorous, but at least it would be private.

The smell of sawdust did not add to the romance of the occasion, but as soon as I saw Special Agent Max Jackson lingering near an elephant-size wide-belt sander that buffed scratches from the White House furniture, we might as well have been in a gondola floating down a Venice canal. Or at the very least walking along the National Mall at night when the Washington, D.C., skyline lit the horizon like a galaxy of stars.

Max's face brightened when he saw me, and I about keeled over right there. God, he was adorable. "Was it hard to get away?" he asked.

Max Jackson was the smartest, most chill guy I'd ever dated, and when he looked down at me with his gorgeous blue eyes that crinkled at the corners, all I wanted to do was run my fingers through his short-cropped curls, pull him close, and kiss him.

And don't even get me started on Max's kissing prowess. Every kiss was DEFCON 1—an all-out nuclear meltdown.

"No prob. You should know I'm an expert at giving my security detail the slip."

"Do I ever." He smiled ruefully. Max had been the head agent on my Secret Service detail until a few weeks ago. He was one of an elite team of young agents trained by the National Security Agency to go undercover where an older agent would stick out like a senior citizen at prom. In other words, he'd been specially trained to guard this National Disaster.

From the get-go, Max and I had butted heads and squabbled until we finally realized the reason sparks flew whenever we were together was because we were crazy about each other. Max asked to be reassigned when his focus shifted from being my bodyguard to being my boyfriend, and now he served on the White House rotation squad. Basically he acted as backup in case one of the regular Secret Service agents was sick or a miscellaneous dignitary needed temporary Secret Service–level security. Maybe it wasn't quite as prestigious as guarding an immediate member of the president's family, but he never complained.

I sensed Max had gotten a lot of flack from his boss about the reassignment. Specially trained agents who were only twenty years old didn't grow on trees, and Max left big shoes to fill. Luckily (or unluckily, depending on my mood), Special Agent Georgina Best had just passed her super-duper First Daughter security instruction. Apparently guarding Tornado (me) required special, intensive training and probably additional hazard pay.

Despite his reassignment, the relationship between Max and me—whatever it was—had to be kept top secret. No one could find out that we were dating. If word leaked, Max would be moved as far away from me as possible. It was strictly forbidden for Secret Service agents to get involved with the protectees. And I wasn't sure how my parents would react to the news that we were together. Mom hated breaking rules. She had also hand-picked Max for my Secret Service detail and was already disappointed when he asked to be reassigned. She might go into a rage if she found out the reason he asked for the reassignment was because he had the hots for me. Besides, my relationship with Max was too important to be dissected in the media spotlight. Paparazzi had a way of killing a mood and crucifying my boyfriends.

So for now it was secret meetings in unromantic places like carpentry shops and storage areas. But when I was with Max, nothing else mattered. It was kind of nice keeping him all to myself . . . sometimes.

"Got you something," Max said. He held out a silvery gift bag.

"That's so sweet. Here, take the scones. They're still warm." I dove excitedly into the bag. "It's . . . pencils."

"Mechanical. So you don't have to worry about broken lead when you fill in the bubbles on the SAT." He beamed at me.

Okay, so Max was also a bit of a nerd. Comes with the whole him-being-a-genius thing—I mean literally a genius. But since he also knew how to fire a government-issued sidearm, held a black belt in karate, and still maintains the record on the Farm's boot-camp obstacle course, he was the coolest nerd on the planet.

"Wait, there's more." Max whipped out a bouquet of lollipops from behind his back. "Pencils for the hard work now, candy for the reward later."

"Aww, Max!" I nudged him with my shoulder. "Thank you."

He nudged back affectionately.

"So, you ready to retake this bad boy?" he asked.

"As ready as I'll ever be, I guess. I studied the *Princeton Review* test prep book until my eyeballs threatened to fall out. And it wasn't easy with the noise coming from the annual Governors' Dinner downstairs, especially when the concert started."

Max raised a brow. "Did you blow off studying to see it?"

"Not this time. No siree. I focused on the task at hand."

What I told Max was true. I did not go down to take a peek at the New Orleans zydeco concert playing at the Governors' Dinner. I'd learned my lesson the last time I skipped studying for the SAT to watch Zed Lassiter jam for my father on his birthday. I had figured I could cram in the Presidential Baby Beast limo on the way to the test, but that plan hit a snag when a Level Two security alert went out as we were leaving for the test center. George made me wait in a secured room under the West Wing portico until the false alarm was over, and in the kerfuffle I'd forgotten my test prep notes in the limo. All the test-taking hints in the world from Max weren't enough to hide the fact that I'd shot myself in the foot, and I wasn't going to do that again. This time I had studied.

"Did you tell your mom you're retaking the test?" Max asked before he bit into a scone.

"No way. She'd kill me. And then my father would sweep up the remains and ask his engineers to rebuild a cyborg daughter, one who didn't eke out worm-low scores on the SAT and disgrace the Abbott family name."

"Isn't it a little early in the morning for melodrama?"

"I'm serious! I've got a lot to live up to: genius parents, blue-blood pedigree, and oh, my mother is the freaking president of the United States."

"Hey, come on. Don't worry so much about disappointing everyone. You're going to do great. I've seen you get out of worse scrapes and come up smelling like a rose. I have faith in you."

"Thanks, Max. That helps. Lots."

"Maybe this will help even more." He settled his lips on mine, and I felt my toes curl. Whoa! Being with Max made my day—my life, actually—even if we had to sneak around. It was totally worth it.

For the next several minutes we forgot about scones and lollipops and SATs and politicians and the Secret Service and hovered in a blissful place, population of two—Max and me. When I was kissing Max, the rest of the world, and all my problems, faded away.

I'd completely mellowed out until I happened to glance at the massive Swiss watch on Max's wrist. Then my world came crashing down.

"Omigod, I'm late!"

Chapter Three

George was waiting for me in the residence hallway when I emerged from the basement stairwell. Her tiny foot tapped in her steel-reinforced boots. "Have a good time?" she inquired.

I hid Max's lollipop bouquet and pencils behind my back. "I, uh, needed to, uh, check something."

"On the ground-floor level?"

"Yeah. I was near the electrical room looking at . . . boiler valves. An upcoming project for physics class."

Boiler valves. Pathetic. She wasn't buying it, obviously. "Hope it was worth it, because you're going to be late for the test. The advance team is onsite now but we can't hold things up for the other students—even for the president's daughter."

I had cajoled my Secret Service detail into keeping my retest a secret from my parents, and for once, they'd sympathized with me. Even George. Guess everyone's afraid of disappointing their parents.

I started to hyperventilate. "I can't be late, George."

She nodded, businesslike. "Then we'll do our best to get you there on time."

For once, George's demanding nature served me well, because the driver of the unmarked car didn't argue when she told him to take the shorter, unauthorized route to the local community college, where the test was being given. We arrived in the parking lot of a 1960s-era cinderblock building with five minutes to spare. No press, either, thank god. I tried to remember Max's test-taking tips: Do the easy questions first, use the process of elimination for questions where I wasn't sure of the answer, and don't get hung up on one question for too long.

I barely registered following George through the maze of classrooms and labs until I was suddenly in a lecture hall packed to the gills with desks. The test proctor looked about eighty years old. He wore super-thick glasses and smelled like licorice, but the Grateful Dead shirt under his blazer was his salvation. After making me empty my pockets of everything but Max's mechanical pencils and a calculator, he herded me to the only seat left in the room.

As I made myself as comfortable as I could in the hard plastic seat, I noticed that right across from me was an overprocessed bleach-blonde who looked like Brittany Whittaker. She was checking herself out in a purse mirror while swabbing gooey, glittery lip gloss over her pouty lips.

Wait a minute, it wasn't a Brittany look-alike; it was the genuine evil article. Ugh.

Brittany Whittaker was my nemesis at Academy of the Potomac—or AOP, as everyone calls it. This was the girl who'd stolen my election platform in order to rig the senior class presidential elections in her favor. Who'd smuggled unflattering photos of me to the press. Who acted like I hailed from Hicksville, USA, because I liked wearing jeans and T-shirts (today's sartorial choice: Psycho Bunny) instead of pastel minis and stilettos.

Brittany's frost-green eyes slid over me and her gloppy-glossed lips curdled into that poo-smelling expression she wore whenever she saw me.

"Abbott," she cooed. Her voice sounded like honey—with a fly drowning in it. "Surprise, surprise. So Mommy President can't get you out of taking the SAT? She gets you out of everything else." She sneered at George, stationed in the doorway.

I ignored the jab at my mom. "What are you doing here, Whittaker? I thought you aced your test." I remembered hearing her brag all over school that her scores were in the highest quadrant and that all the Ivies were after her.

She smirked. "I did. I'm . . . trying to get a higher score."

Oh really. Now it was my turn to smirk. I recognized a white lie when I heard it.

Brittany coolly tossed a lock of flat-ironed hair over her shoulder and checked the oversize LCD screen on the most expensive-looking calculator I'd ever seen, one with about a million buttons. Despite her best efforts she still looked a little uncomfortable. For the first time ever, I felt a teensy iota bad for her.

Sure, she'd made my first few weeks of senior year a living hell. But she'd recently gotten the mother of all comeuppances when she was arrested for assaulting the president of the United States. She pulled my mother's hair at a press conference, thinking it was me wearing a wig. The Secret Service took her down for breaching the president's bubble of security—and those guys don't mess around. Mom had the charges dropped, but the resulting firestorm of bad publicity prompted AOP's student council to strip Brittany of her class presidency and give it to the person who had earned the second-highest number of votes in the election.

Me.

Actually, if I thought about it, things had gone from bad to worse for Brittany. She no longer ruled the school's social calendar nor did her posse of minions follow her around like obedient puppies anymore. I also think her father, Senator Chet Whittaker, leader of the opposition party and my mother's main political adversary, must have grounded her because I hadn't seen her at any school events in a while.

Eep. Am I feeling bad for Brittany? The thing is, she wasn't wrong about me impersonating my mother that night at the American Business Leaders banquet. Her timing had been a little off, that's all. And thank gawd it was, because if she had caught me playing my mom, my mother's presidency would have been finished. Mom and I only agreed to the switch due to a super-secret conference she needed to attend to avoid a possible nuclear war in Africa.

The smell of licorice snapped me back to attention. The proctor was moving through the aisles and had slapped a test booklet in front of me.

Focus, Morgan. Focus. Twenty-five minutes per section does not leave a lot of time for daydreaming.

Mindful of Max's hints, I worked steadily through page after page of algebra equations, feeling semiconfident. Pencils scratched; the clock on the wall ticked. A few coughs and sighs of frustration punctured the quiet. After about fifteen minutes, I lifted my head to uncrick my neck muscles. Next to me, Brittany was staring at her test booklet, and I couldn't help but notice all the bubbles in her test sheet had been filled in.

No way. Not even a genius like Max would be done with an SAT math test after fifteen minutes. And she hadn't even scribbled any problem sets in her test booklet.

Then I noticed Brittany's hand protectively cupping that ridiculous calculator. I could see the letters A, C, D, A glowing between her fingers on the LCD screen.

An awful suspicion sprang into my mind. I'd heard rumors that test grids could be loaded into high-end calculators.

Could Brittany Whittaker be cheating?

The ominous smell of licorice hit me before I heard a throat clearing next to my ear. I jumped. "Keep your eyes on your own test, or I'll have to disqualify you for cheating," the proctor whispered.

"But I . . . "

"You have four minutes left before pencils down," he said firmly.

Crud! I still had about five problem sets to go. I began scribbling, the proctor's eyes burning holes in the side of my head the entire time. When the bell rang for pencils down, I'd managed to finish two more equations.

I leaned back in the chair and heaved a big sigh. One down. Next up: physics.

While the proctor was gathering Scantron sheets,

Brittany leaned over. "Oh my. Look at all the questions you left blank. Have trouble with basic high school algebra, Abbott?"

She laughed. I ground my teeth together.

We had a twenty-minute break between sessions, and I took the opportunity to get some fresh air and try to shake the sick feeling in my stomach.

"How'd it go?" George asked as she escorted me to the grungy patio area off the cafeteria.

"Okay, I guess. I didn't get to finish three of the problem sets."

"It's really hard to finish the whole thing, if I recall. They design the test that way."

"Brittany Whittaker somehow managed," I answered glumly.

"She must be some kind of math whiz then."

"She's not." I bit my lip.

George, somewhat of an expert now on reading my body language, knew something was up. "What is it?"

"I think Brittany was cheating." I explained about the calculator and what I saw in the LCD screen. "But I have no proof. It's just a suspicion anyway."

George's expression didn't change, but her slanty elf eyes went hard.

"Forget about it," I said. "I need to get a snack before the next test. I'm starving."

"Oh? You mean you didn't get a chance to eat any of the

scones you made while you were down in the electrical room this morning?"

"Uh . . . no." I hurried away to the bank of vending machines before she could see me flush.

I bought an energy bar and barely had time to scarf it down before it was time to take the next test. As we took our seats, Brittany pointedly ignored me.

Physics is not my thing at all, and this test was going to be my biggest challenge yet. My previous score was so low, it was embarrassing. I took a couple of deep breaths and focused on the first question. I was barely aware of George moving to the front of the classroom and whispering to the proctor. Brittany's outraged squawk jarred me out of my concentration. "Who do you think you are? I demand you give back my property."

The test proctor loomed over Brittany, holding her calculator and examining the LCD screen. "I need you to come with me, please."

The entire room gasped.

Brittany rose. Scarlet streaked her cheeks, and I thought I saw a shimmer of tears in her eyes. She swiveled toward me. "I'll get you for this," she hissed through her clenched, whitened teeth. "Watch your back, bitch."

Chapter Four

"Serves Brittany right, Morg." My BFF, Hannah Davis, riffled through my closet, throwing outfits that passed her critical judgment on my bed. It was late afternoon, and I'd spent the entire morning draining my brain over SAT questions. Now Hannah had come over to offer a little mental relaxation and some sorely needed fashion advice for the London trip.

She continued, "Little Miss Wonderful tried to game the system by cheating and she got caught. I wouldn't waste one drop of sympathy on her. She wouldn't on you if the situation was reversed."

"I know, I know." I sprawled in my beanbag chair, feeling miserable for some weird reason. Brittany Whittaker got caught cheating because of *me*. And the thing is, I had an inkling of the desperation and pressure she must have felt to get good scores. Everyone growing up in Washington,

D.C., had power-broker parents who didn't settle for second rate—especially in their children.

"Dear gawd. Don't tell me the White House social secretary seriously expects you to wear this in London?" Hannah pulled out a milky-colored dress with hideous navy-blue trim adorning the padded shoulders. "This is like some nightmare uniform from a cruise line."

"She expects it, all right. I'm forbidden from even bringing jeans and T-shirts to London," I said. "I mean, I know I'm not supposed to wear flip-flops to meet the queen, but jeez. Everything she bought is so blah. Thanks for helping me sort through all this, Hans."

"And *thank you* for talking your mom into letting me come along on the trip! We are gonna have a blast!"

"Luckily Mom thinks you're a good influence. She's not taking any chances on me making another classic Morgan Abbott mess, and she expects you to help me not humiliate my country."

"Heh. Little does she know, right?"

"Seriously, Hans. We've got to tone it down when we're over there, or Mom will have my passport revoked."

"Don't worry, there will be no drama on this trip. Just good times. In fact, I've got a heads-up on a killer clubbing hotspot in Piccadilly Circus."

"Hannah! Did Prince Richard text you this morning?"

"He did," she replied modestly, but I could tell she was busting with happiness. Hannah had hooked up with Prince Richard, heir to the British throne and the planet's hottest royal, on his official visit to Washington, D.C., last month and they hadn't stopped texting or webcaming each other since. Not that he could be blamed. Hannah looked stunning today in a ruby-red satin dress that set off her chocolate skin to perfection. My BFF was a born fashionista who knew how to make the most out of her assets, which were considerable. And she helped me make the most of mine, which were difficult to find.

"I can't believe you've snagged a royal," I said, and tried to smile. I was thrilled Hannah was going to get to see Prince Richard again but was also tragically bummed that my time in London would be Max-free if I didn't think of some way to get him assigned to the security entourage for the trip.

"Oh. Mahgawd." Hannah pulled a two-piece business suit in a grotesque shade of oatmeal out of the closet. "Are you sure this isn't one of your mom's?"

"Looks like it could be, doesn't it? Maybe the social secretary thinks I look good in noncolors."

I slipped into the suit and peered at myself in the full-length mirror. I raised my arm, Mom-style. "My fellow Americans. Join me on my important new initiative to eradicate shoulder pads and harem pants in our lifetime."

"Man, it's freaky the way you sound just like her. Hold up." Hannah grabbed a wide tortoiseshell hair band from my dresser and eased it over my head, pushing my choppy bangs back off my forehead with it. A little smoothing, a little fluffing, and she eyed me critically. "Dang, I'm good. May I present President Sara Abbott?"

"Whoa." I took a closer look in the mirror. Hannah was right. Now I *really* looked like my mom.

"I *still* have nightmares about turning into her," I said. "The boring haircut. The sensible suits. Ugh."

"Well, you only look like her," Hannah reassured me. "And sound like her. And act like her when necessary. Typical mother-daughter doppelganger stuff. Your abnormal similarity to each other is completely normal."

"You're not helping." I threw a pillow at her.

She ducked. "And you're freaking out over nothing. Besides, how awesome is it that you can become the president of the United States with just the right outfit, a wig, and my skill with makeup?"

"We need to make sure you use your powers for good instead of evil."

My cell phone chirped, and I glanced at the screen. "It's Max," I said happily. "He's got a fifteen-minute break and wants to see me. Hans, do you mind . . . ?"

"No way! Go get your Max fix. I'll send Rich a text and see if he's up for a chat."

Hannah settled into my beanbag chair while I debated changing out of the fugly suit and back into my jeans and T-shirt. But I didn't want to miss a moment with Max and time was ticking away. Aw, forget it. I'd only be gone a few minutes anyway, I rationalized.

Quickly I texted him to meet me in the Solarium, the third-floor sunroom off the Promenade. We used the sunroom and connecting porch for family barbecues and informal parties. Plus it had the added bonus of being away from the main hub of activity on the floor. Perfect for a rendezvous with Max.

I slipped out of my room wearing the suit and nearly tripped over a bronze bust of Teddy Roosevelt sitting in the middle of the hall. The furniture had been pulled away from the wall for the weekly cleaning of the residence wing common areas. The scent of Brasso and lemon furniture polish tickled my nose.

Suddenly, a member of the housekeeping staff emerged from one of the spare bedrooms. "Afternoon, Madam President," she said as she breezed by me.

I opened my mouth to correct her, but she'd already ducked into another room. Short of chasing her down to set her straight, I'd have to let it go.

I tiptoed down the center hall, dodging a vacuum cleaner and janitor's cart and hoping to avoid being seen by whoever happened to be on duty at the Secret Service desk at the end of the hall.

Two agents stood at the desk. My heart stalled. Max! God, he looked so cute in his boring brown business suit. I couldn't wait to get my hands on him. . . .

And there was George standing right next to him.

Chapter Five

My step faltered. George, yikes! I did not want her interfering and asking a bunch of questions about why Max was waiting for me. Should I abort the mission, as Max would say?

In that split second of indecision, George looked beyond Max and saw me.

"Good afternoon, Madam President," she said deferentially.

Ha! She thought I was my mom. Maybe I could take advantage of the situation.

I straightened my shoulders and told myself to look presidential. I modulated my voice to my mother's measured tones. "Good afternoon, Agent Best. Agent Jackson."

"Good afternoo . . . " Max did a double take.

I plastered a pleasant smile on my face and nodded at him encouragingly.

" . . . noon, Madam President." Max instantly recovered from his surprise. "Heading down to the Oval Office?"

"Uh . . . yes?" I clued into Max's imperceptible nod.

"Perhaps you'd like to use the stairwell at the other end of the hall," he continued. "Housekeeping is shampooing the carpeting on this end."

I glanced over my shoulder. Near the door to the linen room, the housekeeper I'd seen earlier fiddled with extension cords and an upright carpet cleaner.

"Good idea, Agent Jackson. I'll do just that. Carry on."

With a brisk nod to George, who'd been examining me with an expressionless face, I headed back down the hall. When I reached the entrance of the ramp leading up to the Solarium, I glanced behind to make sure I was hidden from the Secret Service station. Then I ducked inside. Safe!

The Solarium's skylights and panoramic windows gave the room an airy feeling. The room had always been a favorite of mine, and I'd even held my sweet sixteen birthday party out on the Promenade, which overlooked the South Lawn. My dad had booked Arcada, the hottest boy band at the time, to give me and my friends a kick-ass concert. It was amazing.

After the party (okay, maybe the impromptu mosh pit trashed the room *just a smidge*), Mom had the room redecorated in eco-friendly paints and fabrics. It lived up to strict environmental standards. But the Solarium's soothing earth tones and wind chimes couldn't calm me. I was too worried that George had figured out who I was and was going to ruin my interlude with Max.

As that horrible thought tumbled through my head, a male voice echoed up from the Solarium's ramp. "Hello?"

"Max!" I rushed him as soon as he entered the room.

He let out an *oof* when our bodies collided. "Okay, Morgan. I'm not sure I want to know, but I guess I have to ask. Why are you pretending to be your mother?"

"I wasn't really trying to impersonate Mom. Hannah and I were messing around, trying on my mom-inspired fashions for London, when I got your text . . . anyway, forget it," I said as the confusion grew on his face. "George was fooled and will leave us alone. How much time do we have?"

He glanced at his watch. "About five minutes. I'm sorry I got hung up at Bubble Central."

"Five minutes?" Was that all? I grabbed him by the tie and pulled his mouth to mine.

After a moment, he came up for air. "Whoa. It's weird to be kissing the president." He leaned back, still holding me in his strong arms.

I smacked him on his well-toned bicep. Very well toned. Mmm. Whodathunk that such a hot bod lurked under a government-issue suit? "Knock it off." I smiled a mischievous smile. "And that's an order!"

I pulled him close again.

"I can't believe I'm dating the president's daughter," he murmured. "You could have any guy you want. Why me?"

"Oh, let's see. For starters because you're adorable, smart, a great dancer, and an even better kisser."

"Maybe we'd better practice that last bit again." He grinned.

"Hang on. I think I hear someone coming."

In a flash, boyfriend Max disappeared and Secret Service Agent Max Jackson reappeared. He and I sprang apart, and I dove into the butler's pantry just as someone entered the room.

"Oh!" said a female voice I didn't recognize. "I didn't know anyone was in here." A cleaning bucket rattled, and I caught a whiff of pine-scented cleanser.

"Sweeping the room for a routine security check," Max said.

Good thinking, Max! I cheered silently.

"That's strange," I heard her say. "The head housekeeper didn't mention any security sweeps happening in the residence today."

"I should be finished in ten minutes or so," Max said firmly.

"I guess I'll come back later" was the reply. "Or I could get started vacuuming while you finish your sweep—"

"It would be best if you came back later."

A pause, maybe a frustrated sigh, some footsteps. A tense moment, and then Max poked his head into the butler's pantry. "Okay in there?"

"Fine. We have about twenty-five cans of Clamato stored here, in case you're interested."

Max let out a huge breath. "That was a close call."

"We've been in worse situations."

"It's not over yet. I'll leave first. You wait three minutes before you leave. I should be downstairs by then."

"Check. But first, Agent Jackson, the president's daughter has a request."

He stroked my cheek with the back of his hand. "And that is?"

I nuzzled into his palm. "One more kiss."

A moment later, Max slipped out of the Solarium, smoothing his hair and straightening his tie. Dreamily I wandered around the room until I thought about three minutes had passed, enough time for Max to make his escape.

As I left the room, I should have been paying attention instead of thinking about how good Max's new aftershave smelled. I didn't check to make sure the coast was clear like I normally would have. Unfortunately, at the end of the hall, a member of the housekeeping staff who I didn't recognize was dusting the Coolidge-era paperweight memorabilia collection. Was this the same person who'd almost caught us? Uh-oh. Maybe I was only imagining the speculative expression on her face.

I straightened my spine and walked with my mother's trademark quickstep. "Good afternoon," I said to the housekeeper as I passed her.

She nodded deferentially. "Afternoon, Madam President."

Mom would have added a thoughtful comment. She always treated staff members with extreme courtesy. "You're, ah, doing an excellent job dusting," I said, then winced. That was pretty lame.

But the housekeeper beamed. "Thank you, ma'am. I hope the shampooer won't disturb Morgan when we run it by her bedroom door. The motor can get loud."

I could still feel the pressure of Max's lips against mine. "It won't. I can say with complete confidence that Morgan's got other things on her mind right now."

Chapter Six

At school on Monday, Hannah met me at our lockers before study hall. "Ready to take up the reins of power at the first student council meeting?" she quipped. "AOP's got a new prez, and she's ready to kick booty."

"You're in a good mood this morning," I said. "Must have to do with that epic IM chat with Prince Richard."

"I'm in as good a mood as you were in after your make-out session with Max on Saturday."

We giggled.

"Better get to work," I said, and grabbed out of my locker a spiral notebook that I'd designated as the official log of AOP's senior class president. *Put everything in writing,* Mom always said. I was determined to go by the book, too. Now that I was senior class president, I wasn't taking any chances. We were already midway through the first semester and the class hadn't done any fund-raising for prom, our graduation party, or worse, any philanthropic initiatives.

That was going to change.

I strode into the biology lab, which doubled as our meeting room.

Jeong Nguyn hummed "Hail to the Chief." "All rise for our new president."

"Knock it off." I blushed as the senior council applauded. "Let's get started, we've got a lot to cover today."

"You mean we're going to get some actual work done instead of bitching about how busy the class president is?" asked Carl, the swim captain who represented the Athletics Council.

Ouch. Slam on Brittany.

I was tempted to join in but remembered another one of Mom's golden rules: Don't badmouth your political enemies. Even though I *reeeally* wanted to take the opportunity to do just that.

I rose above my urge to snark, and at that moment, Brittany Whittaker waltzed into the lab.

"Sorry I'm late," she said coolly into the pool of shocked silence. "I hope I didn't miss anything."

"Uh, no." Everyone looked as puzzled as I felt. What was she doing here? *Don't make a scene. . . .* "We're just getting down to business."

She gave a gracious wave of her hand. "Carry on, Morgan."

"Oookay. Let's start with the treasurer's report."

Mya Boskovitch, the head cheerleader, opened her laptop and brought up a spreadsheet. Mya and I had had our differences, especially where my former boyfriend Konner was concerned, but there was no denying she had a head for business. The cheerleaders were the most solvent activities group at AOP.

"Our balance is seventy-five dollars and eighteen cents," she said.

My mouth fell open. "That's it?"

"I just paid a huge florist bill for our homecoming dance," Mya said with a pointed look at Brittany. "So we're gutted."

"Wow." I was reeling, but shook it off in a hurry as the rest of the student council was looking at me with a bleak expression and mentally waving good-bye to our prom and graduation party. Everyone except for Brittany, that is. She fingered the gold chain around her neck and kept her face carefully blank, eyes hooded.

Like a cobra.

"Okay, brainstorm," I said. "We've got to figure out a way to raise a decent amount of money in a short amount of time if we want to put deposits down for our prom venue."

"What about a car wash?" Carl suggested.

"Bake sale?" Mya offered.

"Good, good." I started writing the suggestions in my notebook. "Keep 'em coming."

"We could do a raffle," Hannah suggested. "Ask local businesses to donate items to auction off."

Brittany's sugary voice cut across the babble. "All those ideas are lame. We need at least five grand to hold both a prom and a graduation party. A bake sale or auction isn't going to raise enough cash to put down a deposit, let alone fund the events."

"Well, since you're the one who blew our entire treasury on *flowers* for homecoming, do you have any better ideas?" I shot back.

"As a matter of fact, I do."

Uh-oh. I sensed too late that I was walking into a trap.

"Why don't you host a private party at the White House?"

No. Nonononono. "How would that raise money?"

"We could charge a 'donation' for everyone who wanted to attend. It'll be huge, especially if your mother is there. People will pay good money to socialize with the president and to see the sections of the White House not open to the public. Or so I hear."

"Yeah, my dad would pay big bucks to have me party

with the president," Carl said.

"I'm not sure my mom would go for that—" I began, but I was drowned out by enthusiastic yells of approval from everyone else.

"God, we'd make all we need and then some to get our philanthropy slate off the ground," Mya said. "Plus, is it true the White House has its own bowling alley?"

"Hang on, hang on!" I shouted, but no one listened to me. The whole meeting had gone completely off the rails. Everyone was squealing with excitement over the prospect of partying at the White House and solving our financial dilemmas in one fell swoop. But how was I supposed to talk my mom into this?

From her seat, Brittany sent me the evilest smile ever.

After the meeting, I was moodily crunching through a bag of Cheetos and thinking about the right approach to take with my mom over this senior class fund-raiser situation, when I saw Ms. Gibson, AOP's guidance counselor, heading straight for me. I quickly stuffed the bag inside my three-ring binder and stopped midchew. Eating in the halls was an infraction, and I didn't need any more demerits in my file.

"Morgan, I need to see you in my office," Gibson said in her scary, don't-even-think-about-giving-me-any-lip voice.

I nodded, hoping my mouth wasn't covered in that tell-tale neon-orange Cheeto dust.

"Right now," she added.

Nod.

Her Angelina Jolie mouth tightened suspiciously, but she headed into her office without another word or glance behind her, obviously expecting me to follow obediently. Which I did. No one disobeyed Gibson.

No sooner had she settled behind her freakishly neat desk—a coffee mug at a convenient distance from her computer mouse, of course—did she attack. "What are your college plans, Morgan?"

"Uh . . . to get into one? Hopefully."

"The AOP phones have been ringing off the hook from college admissions offices around the world."

"They are? That's weird."

She sighed in frustration. "They're asking about *you*."

"Me?" The synthetic flavoring chemicals in the Cheetos must have slowed my brain's comprehension function. I knew it wasn't a good idea to look so vacant in front of Gibson, but I was honestly confused. My grades sucked. My SAT scores were stunningly average, at best. "Why?"

Gibson gave me her patented "Is this girl for real?" look. "Because you're the daughter of the president of the United States, that's why. It's great publicity for the university that lands you. Plus, they probably think they could get your mother to speak at convocations or graduation."

Ha! Well, the joke's on them if they think they could leverage my mom into doing something she doesn't want to do.

Gibson leaned forward over her desk and lowered her voice. "I've been offered all kinds of bribes and perks if I can persuade you to attend this college or that." She sat back and took a sip from her mug. "Of course, I refused. But that doesn't stop us from needing to have a conversation about your future. I noticed you haven't started the application process yet."

"Nope. To be honest, I haven't given it much consideration. I thought I had some time."

"The time to start applying for early admissions is now. We need to get your transcripts ordered, letters of recommendation written, et cetera."

"But I have no idea what I want to do with my life. Shouldn't I get that basic fact under control before I start applying to universities?"

"Morgan, no one is asking you to make a decision on your future right now. College is for testing your boundaries and discovering new talents. Most people start college with one major in mind, and then find out they want to explore other disciplines. And that's okay. You'll have a chance to decide what's right for you."

I heaved a big sigh. "Well, that's a relief."

Gibson went on. "You know, when I was at Cornell, I tried all sorts of things: biology, musicology, public affairs, ballroom dancing—"

"Ballroom dancing? Like, doing the rumba with feathers and stuff?" I giggled. Tomb Raider Gibson dancing to the cha-cha-cha? No way!

"It wasn't like that." She drew herself up defensively. "But the point is, I expanded my horizons while I was away at college, which led to my falling in love with education. And here I am today."

"That's . . . uh . . . fantastic."

"Cornell has a great reputation and you would get a top-notch education there." Gibson took a sip from her mug. And I suddenly noticed Cornell's distinctive red seal plastered on its side.

"You think about it," she said. "Wherever you decide to go, I'm sure the institution will admit you. But this is not a time to let your grades slip even lower than they already are. You still have to have a diploma from *this* institution."

"Okay. I'll think about it."

I left her office feeling hollow. I wanted to be admitted into a college based on my own merits, not because I was the president's daughter. I hated everyone sucking up to me because my last name was Abbott. Or because I was a handy tool to get in good with my mother.

Instead of making me feel better about college, the conversation with Gibson added another level to the pressure already on me. I wished everyone would back off and let *me* figure out what I wanted to do with the rest of my life.

Chapter Seven

On my way home from school in the Baby Beast, my cell phone chirped. I glanced at the screen. Great. Mom wanted to see me in the Oval Office as soon as I got in. That couldn't be good.

George escorted me into the protective security bubble of the West Wing, then bailed to change out of her "school uniform" (jeans and a flannel shirt, which made her look about fourteen years old), and I dragged myself down the hall past the portraits of Truman and Eisenhower toward the Oval Office. As I reached the door to the executive suite, Humberto Morales swung into the corridor. "Morgan, just a sec," he said.

"Whatever it is, I didn't do it," I replied automatically.

Humberto gave me a mock wince. He'd been putting out fires for Mom ever since she'd become president, but he made no secret of the fact that the kind of trouble I got into was far worse than anything he'd had to deal with as Mom's right-hand man. *Hey, just because I impersonate the president occasionally is no reason for Humberto to stock up on Rogaine,* I thought grouchily.

"Am I in trouble?" I asked.

"No, no. At least, nothing I know of."

Whew.

"I heard that you were taking your SAT," he went on.

I nodded, confused. Why would Humberto care that I had taken my SAT? Unless he had inside information that I'd gotten super-low scores again and was about to embarrass my mom.

The headline flashed through my head:

MORGAN ABBOTT'S EPIC FAILURE: WILL SHE HAVE TO REPEAT HIGH SCHOOL?

"I was wondering if you've given any thought to where you want to go to college."

College? *Again?* Why couldn't everyone stop bugging me about it?

"Not really . . ."

"Northwestern University happens to have a great law school."

"Northwestern? In Chicago?"

"It's my alma mater," he said modestly. "I took law prep there. I really think you should consider the legal profession. You'd make a great lawyer someday."

I felt my jaw sag. Me, a lawyer? Sure, I could talk my way out of anything if I had to, but the thought of wading through legal briefs and tort cases almost made me break out in hives.

Humberto's BlackBerry chirped. "I've got to run," he said. "You think about it. If you're interested, I can make a call. I know a few members on the board of trustees. Plus I'm the chair of my alumni association." He began trotting down the hall and soon disappeared into the Cabinet Room.

I shook my head. *That* was weird.

I headed into the Executive Suite. "Wassup, Pads?" I said to Padma, Mom's executive assistant. "Got any toffees?"

"Help yourself." Padma pushed the candy jar on her desk toward me and I dug in. "Word of warning," she whispered. "Sara's not a happy camper right now."

Teeth glued together by caramelized sugar, I nodded. Usually when I got called into the Oval Office, it involved me being in trouble.

Padma opened the connecting door leading into the Oval Office, and I entered. Seated at the Resolute Desk, Mom frowned into her specially developed Abbott Technologies laptop. The pastel lavender suit she was wearing actually looked good on Mom because of the smart Chinese collar that showed a teensy hint of style for once. She'd let her basic bob haircut grow a little longer, and if she wasn't my mom, I'd think she was a college intern playing Pretend to Be the Boss at the president's desk.

"What is this, Morgan?" she asked. The serious tone of her voice instantly set me on alert.

I sighed. "Clue me in."

She turned her computer toward me. On the high-res monitor, the headline on one of D.C.'s most popular political blogs blared: PRESIDENT ABBOTT CAUGHT IN THE ARMS OF A YOUNG AGENT—DEVELOPING!!!!!

I felt my heart stop.

Hands shaking, I pulled the laptop closer. "Sources inside the White House reveal that the youthful President Abbott has been seen cavorting with a young Secret Service agent. Rumor? Or truth? We'll keep digging."

Mom's face was stony. "Do you know anything about this?"

Horrified, I stalled for time by collapsing on one of the overstuffed sofas that flanked the Presidential Seal woven on the rug. I wanted to tell Mom that Max and I were a thing, but I couldn't risk Max's career.

I gave a shaky laugh. "You know how the press twists everything around," I managed to squeak out.

"So you haven't been impersonating the president lately?"

Avoid the subject without denying. "Maybe someone saw you talking to Parker and got the wrong idea."

"Maybe. Or maybe you're not telling me something."

"Like what?"

"Like you have a boyfriend?"

Urk. No way could I tell mom about Max. But I haaaated lying to her. So I hedged. "I'm not interested in anyone at school right now, no."

Mom laid down one of her penetrating stares that stripped the skin off heads of state. She wasn't buying it. I needed to think fast before she asked me the question I could almost see forming in that presidential brain of hers. Redirect! Redirect!

"Besides, I'm so busy right now," I said. "I've got a major problem, and I hope you can help me out."

I explained about the depleted senior-class treasury thanks to Brittany Whittaker's brief reign of terror, and the idea of having a fund-raising party at the White House.

"I don't think it's a good idea," I said hastily when I caught the expression on Mom's face. "But I have to agree with the rest of the class officers that it would raise what we need quickly so we can concentrate on our initiatives instead of worrying about the budget."

"Spoken like a true elected official," Mom remarked.

I perked up. "Is that good?"

"It's good, sweetie. You're thinking of how to achieve the goal in the most effective way. All right, I agree. But you'll have to clear it with the security team and the social secretary first. There will be restrictions, you know."

"No problem, Mom." I got up and gave her a hug. "Thanks for agreeing. I know this isn't your thing."

She hugged me back tightly. "Well, I'm not just the president, I'm also a parent. Besides, I owe you one for helping with the African peace talks. We're a team, remember?"

"Yeah. A pretty kick-ass one at that."

"I think so, too. And I've been thinking, when we're in London, I'd like you to spend a day with me. I think you'd make a great politician."

I laughed. "A politician? I've already been the president of the United States. Anything else is a demotion."

Mom chuckled.

"Sure, Mom. I'd love to hang with you in London."

"As for this internet rumor," she sighed, "I guess the best course of action is to let it die for lack of oxygen. We can't respond to every random item some blogger decides to post."

"Excellent decision, Mom."

I headed to the door, feeling great. Not only did I manage to dodge the question about Max, but I'd talked Mom into having the fund-raiser at the White House. I gave myself a pat on the back.

I had my hand on the brass knob, *almost* free and clear, when Mom's voice stopped me. "Oh, by the way, have you given any thought to prospective colleges? The window for applications is upon us, you know."

What was going on? This was the third conversation about colleges I'd had today. I was soooo sick of it!

"I, uh, have some ideas in mind," I hedged.

"Because my alma mater would be perfect for you," Mom said.

Harvard? Yeah, right. Like that place would admit a screwup with marginal grades like me. Even with presidential backing, I knew it wouldn't happen.

"I guess I could give it a look," I said unenthusiastically.

"Excellent." Mom beamed. "Let me know when, and I'll arrange a tour."

I gave a sickly smile and got the hell out of there before Mom could launch into stories of her wild days sitting in Harvard's Lamont Library and leading her debate team to a rousing discussion of international economic policies or something.

If Mom thought I'd turn into a brainiac overnight, she was more optimistic than I thought.

Chapter Eight

"**Nigel, what if we go Mexican with this?** It's a fiesta, right? Mockeritas, nachos, tapas, stuff like that."

Nigel Bellingham, the White House's executive chef, grinned. The killer smell of braising meat and fresh chopped herbs penetrated the air in his tiny office adjacent to the White House kitchens, where he and I were meeting. It had been a week since my mom had given permission to hold the fund-raising party at the White House, and planning the menu was going to be the best part of the event.

"Technically, tapas are Spanish, luvvie, but I like where you're headed," Nigel said. "You want finger foods for your party so the guests are able to stay mobile."

"Yeah, that's it. I don't want anyone plopping down in their cliques and gossiping."

Nigel eyed the menu I'd scribbled on a piece of loose-leaf notebook paper. "You've got a natural flair for planning an event, luv. Let me talk this over with the staff, and we'll see what we can do to make your party even more smashing."

"Thanks, Nige." I beamed. I loved hanging out with Nigel. The creative chaos of the White House kitchens energized me, and I loved seeing what the gifted chefs created even given the security restrictions of cooking for the most powerful people in the world. Food had to be inspected by the Secret Service in a special procurement procedure, and if it didn't clear in time to be served to the president, then oh well—the staff had to improvise. I got a charge out of seeing how creative they could be with food at the last minute.

Speaking of security, George poked her head into the office, hand cupped over her ear-com so she could hear over the flames and curses erupting near the burners. "Agent Jackson says you have a visitor moving through the security chain, Morgan. Where do you want her to go?"

The mention of Max's name made my heart do a little square dance. Then I remembered. . . . "Oh god, is Hannah here already? I've totally lost track of time!"

"Big shock," I thought I heard George mutter.

"I'll meet her upstairs in the residence. Are we good, Nige?"

"Ducky." Nigel folded my menu and tucked it into the pocket of his chef's smock. "Don't worry about a thing. The party will be a smash."

If only I could take his words to heart. Because with me in the driver's seat, there was a good chance of a pile-up somewhere along the road.

George left me once I entered the residence wing, and I found Hannah waiting for me in the kitchen so we could spread out. She was helping me plan the party itinerary, and we had to have basically every second accounted for before the White House social staff and the Secret Service would approve it.

"Hey, Morg." Hannah greeted me by waving a purple sparkle pen over the screen of her mini laptop. "This party is really shaping up! Looks like every single senior is coming. Not only that, they all bought tickets for the behind-the-scenes tour with your mom. And the mini concert with Cin'Qua didn't hurt, either."

Cin'Qua was a scorching-hot hip-hop singer whose latest single, "Shake That," dominated the airwaves. He'd agreed to perform at my party if my dad would hang out with him afterward and show him the latest electronic gadgetry from Abbott Technology's experimental lab.

"So? How do the financials look?" I asked.

Hannah tapped at the computer and studied the spreadsheet. "Let's just say the class treasury is solvent again."

"Excellent. My stomach ulcers will be worth it in the

end." Planning the fund-raiser had pretty much consumed all my free time over the past week. I needed to get this right, not only to help the senior class but also to prove to myself and my classmates that I was leadership material.

"Let's go over everything again," I said.

She groaned. "Relax, Morgan. The situation is under control. Killer food, check. Awesome entertainment, check. Sold-out tickets, check. This event will be the biggest fund-raising success in the history of AOP's senior class. You'll see."

Despite the fun of picking out a cute ethnic-inspired dress for the party—with adorable strappy heels, of course—by the time the day of the event rolled around, my stress levels had reached critical mass. But I'd been dealing with pressure my whole life and knew that the way to cope was to block out the disaster scenarios and focus on a positive outcome. No matter what, tonight was sure to be a night to remember.

The Yellow Oval Room in the residence wing looked fantastic. When the White House social team tackles a job, look out. They transformed the old-fashioned decor by moving out the traditional furniture and creating a fiesta wonderland. Twinkly lights twisted around real mini palm trees, and the buffet table had been staged to look like a beach cabana. Flameless candles on the tables brought a touch of Cabo San Lucas to the ambiance. The French windows opened up to the Truman Balcony, which overlooked the Washington, D.C., skyline. A mini stage had been set up on the balcony with speakers and all sorts of equipment for Cin'Qua's number, which was sure to be an unbelievable spectacle with the Washington and Jefferson memorials lit up in the distance.

The only thing that would make tonight perfect would be if Brittany Whittaker got stuck in traffic or suffered a massive wardrobe malfunction that made it impossible for her to attend the party. No refunds would be issued on her ticket, either.

"Ready for the party, Morgan?" Max's voice broke through my concentration.

Max.

I forced my mouth into a smile to hide my anxiety. "Yup. Everything's going to be great."

Max had been assigned to security for my party, which meant he'd be close by. So close, and yet so far. He wore his boring brown suit again, but the nondescript threads made him even more adorable, if that was possible. I wanted to head straight into his arms, despite all the staffers weaving in and out of the room.

He leaned toward me, keeping his hands firmly clasped

behind him, Secret Service style. No one looking at us would suspect that we wanted to rip into each other.

"You look beautiful," he murmured.

Tingles sparked my nerve endings. I really wanted him to kiss me. Before I could stop myself, I lifted my face up to his. He inched forward, too. . . .

"Hey, Morg!"

Hannah's voice cut between us. We sprang apart.

Hannah glanced from me to Max and back to me again, trying not to laugh at our gooey expressions. "I'm not *interrupting* anything, am I?"

"Nope. Nothing at all." Max and I exchanged rueful looks. Close call!

Hannah looked kick-awesome in a Mexican print skirt, embroidered peasant blouse, and about a million bangles on her wrists, an ensemble only Hannah could pull off. Somehow she always managed to turn a gimmick into high fashion. "The place looks fantabulous. Kudos to the White House staff for rocking it out."

A stir rippled among staff members. Parker, Mom's Secret Service agent, entered, immediately followed by Mom wearing a beige pantsuit. At least she tried to be jaunty by jazzing up her look with the Huichol Indian friendship bracelet she'd gotten from the president of Mexico on her last state visit to the country. Dad followed, looking fly in jeans, a bespoke fitted shirt, and snakeskin cowboy boots. Sauntering next to him, speaking with animation was—

"Omigod! It's Cin'Qua!" Hannah about lost her cool when she laid eyes on the hip-hop star wearing several layers of baggy gangsta clothes and about twenty pounds of gold chains. George trailed Cin'Qua, her eyes sweeping the room in Secret Service overdrive. I'd gotten her assigned to Cin'Qua for tonight since Max told me he was her favorite singer. Who knew Little Miss Pixie liked hip-hop? It also meant that I wouldn't be tripping over her all night.

Mom headed over to me. "Is it showtime yet, honey? Hi there, Agent Jackson. Hannah."

"Madam President." Max morphed into his professional Secret Service persona. The president's arrival meant that he had to get back to work. To me, he said formally, "Good luck tonight, Morgan."

"Thanks, Max."

I watched him head to the security checkpoint station downstairs at the base of the grand staircase and squelched a wistful expression.

Meanwhile, my super-cool bud Hannah was fangirling out over meeting the rap singer. "I've downloaded all your albums," she squeaked. "It's an honor to meet you in person."

"Yo," came Cin'Qua's reply.

Hannah continued to gaze at Cin'Qua in adoration. "Yo," she repeated dreamily.

He edged away. "Maybe I should start my sound checks," he said to Dad and George.

"Good idea," Dad replied, amused. "I'll show you the stage." George cleared the way to the balcony in hyper-professional mode. Hannah followed them at a discreet distance. *OMG*, she mouthed at me.

I turned to Mom. "It's almost time for the guests to arrive." I gave her a hug. "Thanks for doing this. I know it's a big time-suck."

"No problem, sweetie. It'll be fun showing your class-mates around the White House. *If* they can tear themselves away from jamming to 'Shake That.'"

"How do you know that song?"

"I haven't been living in a cave for the last six months, honey. I get briefed on pop culture."

She threw an awkward gangsta sign, and I busted up. Sometimes my mom could be so cool.

One of the event management junior staffers approached. "Guests are arriving, Morgan."

I turned eagerly to the doorway, ready to be a good hostess. . . .

Then Brittany Whittaker glided in.

Gag. Whittaker *would* be the first to arrive. Figures.

She'd poured her slender body into a zipper-fronted white jumpsuit that made her look insanely stacked, and she towered over me in four-inch platform wedges. Her eyes zoomed around the room until they landed on my mom. Instantly she tottered over to us.

Stationed in a discreet but visible corner of the room, Mom's head agent, Parker, pressed the com on his lapel. Mom shook her head at him. I knew that Mom had issued a special order to drop Brittany from the Watch List kept by the Secret Service against possible threats to the president. "I couldn't let her go through life with that hanging over her head," Mom had said when I told her I wanted to keep the White House a Brittany-free environment. "She learned her lesson."

"President Abbott," Brittany began with a fake-humble smile. "It's such an honor to be here. And what a lovely shade of brown you're wearing. It really sets off your coloring." Her eyes darted to me in my colorful print dress. "Sometimes subtlety works best in fashion, don't you think?"

"What a lovely compliment, Brittany. Thank you. And don't worry, I'm not holding any press conferences tonight."

Mom! Oh *snap!*

"I want to apologize again for what happened. I thought, well, I was . . ." Brittany spluttered.

"We've put that unfortunate incident behind us," Mom interjected, saving Brittany from more humiliation.

Brittany turned an ugly shade of purple and slithered away.

"I probably shouldn't have said that, huh?" Mom remarked when Brittany was out of earshot.

I started giggling. "Probably not. But I loved it!"

Now the room really started filling up with my classmates. They oohed over the decorations, and some, holding copies of Cin'Qua's latest *Rolling Stone* magazine cover, headed straight to the balcony to snag an autograph. George organized the fans in a line and—wait—did her Secret Service eyes linger for a moment too long on Cin'Qua's booty? George was full of surprises.

"The party certainly has started," Mom said. "When do you want to begin the tours, honey?"

"Why don't we let everyone run through the buffet line once first," I said. "People will be less antsy on a full stomach."

"Sounds like a plan."

The party revved up. People gushed about the food, and especially my mango salsa and smoked chipotle flautas. Mom started the tours.

So far, so good. Every so often, I spied Max when he took his turn to perform routine security sweeps of the event.

At one point I caught him looking longingly at me. Then he did that magic Secret Service thing where he blended into the crowd and disappeared. I wished he could be right by my side as my boyfriend tonight—no secrets, no hiding.

I surveyed the guests again, eager to distract myself from the strange loneliness I was feeling in a room full of people. Cin'Qua started to play. Jonas, the horndog captain of the tennis squad, was hitting on Mya while she ignored Konner, my ex, who was checking himself out in the antique mirror hanging over the unlit fireplace. The buffet table was already a wreck. Jeong and Carl were hanging there, scraping up mango salsa with Nigel's homemade tortilla chips. "This party's the bomb, Morgan," Carl said, mouth full.

"Yeah, and your mom's tour was so cool," Jeong added. "Whodathunk the president of the United States was so funny? She showed us your dad's nunchuk collection in the gym, and I couldn't stop cracking up when she said she had to borrow them every so often to break a Congressional filibuster."

"That was classic!" Carl busted up.

"Ha ha." I scanned the room again. I couldn't put my finger on it but something was wrong. "Hey, have you guys seen Brittany?"

They shook their heads. "And that's a bad thing

because . . . ?" Jeong asked.

"It's better to see the snake than wonder where it is," I said.

"Good luck with that." Carl gave a sympathetic shrug and went back to his chips.

I headed to the balcony, which was jammed with a White House–style mosh pit. Hannah was out there, her normally pulled-together outfit seriously messed up from her spazzing out in the front row of Cin'Qua's concert.

A sick feeling was developing in my stomach. If someone wanted to see me fail, it would be Brittany. She was up to something. I just knew it.

I searched the Red Room, the Map Room, and the other rooms the White House security team had authorized access to. No dice.

In the family residence hallway, that suspicious feeling persisted, and on a hunch, I headed to my bedroom.

"What. The. *Hell*?" I yelled.

Brittany Whittaker was *in my bedroom*.

Blind fury gripped me and I didn't care if I would get arrested for assault, I wanted to rip her flat-ironed hair out of her skull by the fistful. "You've got two seconds to explain what you think you're doing in here. Then I'm calling Secret Service to have them remove an intruder, and send your ass back to the D.C. jail."

"Chill, Abbott. Chill." Brittany kept a good game face, but her cheeks turned pink when I mentioned jail time. "I got lost, that's all. Trying to find the bathroom. It's confusing here, you know."

"Gimme a break. You're snooping."

"*Pfft*. You're high on your own ego, *First Daughter*." She spat the last two words. "Living in the White House has turned you into a spoiled brat."

My hands curled into fists. No one called me a spoiled brat and got away with it. "Oh yeah? I don't need any Special Forces to throw you out of my room. This *brat* can take out her own trash."

"I'm going, I'm going," she said hurriedly. Maybe the manic gleam of anger in my eye had finally penetrated her pea brain.

"And if you go outside the perimeter again, I'm having the Secret Service haul you off. Good luck explaining to your dad how you wound up on the Watch List *again*. He must get sick of having to bail you out."

She opened her mouth to say something but thought better of it and left.

It took me a few minutes to calm down. God! My room felt polluted. Her floral perfume stank up the joint.

I went to my dresser to make sure she hadn't rifled through my things. The surface seemed unchanged. Earrings and necklaces jumbled across the top. A notebook of recipes that I'd cribbed from the White House kitchens lay open to the same page I'd left it. Hmm. Something still didn't feel right.

I went to my closet and threw the door open. My shoes were piled up on the floor as usual and didn't seem disturbed. Nor did my clothes.

Hold up.

On the floor of my closet, buried in a corner, was a plastic storage box of photos. The plastic clip sealing the box was open.

The sick feeling in my stomach intensified.

I opened the lid. On top of a pile of photos lay a snapshot of Max and me from when we'd stolen an afternoon to walk around Constitution Gardens. Cheeks pressed together, we'd smiled cheesily into my cell-phone camera. I'd printed it because I loved the image so much, but I was afraid to leave it on my phone in case someone found it.

But someone did anyway.

I tried not to run as I slipped down the grand staircase to the security checkpoint on the first floor. The hallway was deserted except for Max, who sat at the desk and fiddled with the dials of a security camera, clearly bored.

"Max!" I hissed, beckoning him to the shadow of the staircase. "I think Brittany knows about us."

"What? How?"

I told him about finding her in my room and how the photo box in my closet had been rummaged through.

"But you have no proof of that, Morg. You could have forgotten to close the box yourself."

"Hey! Whose side are you on?"

"Yours, you know that." He shifted closer and I could smell his aftershave. "Always."

Guh. When Max looked at me like that, I forgot about everything but the way his lips felt against mine.

His attention locked on my mouth. I bit my lower lip. "This is driving me nuts."

"What is?" Rarely had I seen Max forget his surroundings, and it jolted me to think that I was making him as crazy as he was making me.

"Seeing you looking so beautiful. Missing you."

"I miss you, too." I leaned closer, expecting him to pull back and be the rational one.

Instead, he swept in for an intense kiss.

A flash of light arced between us. We jumped apart.

"Tsk, tsk." Brittany Whittaker glanced at the cell phone in her hand. The image of Max and me kissing filled the screen. "I bet Mommy Dearest would be thrilled to find out her daughter is a sleazy skank. Don't you think, Morgan?"

Chapter Nine

I lunged for the cell phone, but Brittany jerked it away. "Don't do that," she warned. "I might accidentally hit the Send key and who knows where this photo might go. The *D.C. Gadfly*, or maybe the *Washington Post*'s gossip page. Or perhaps to my father's home computer. I'm sure he'd like to discuss this display of unprofessionalism with the head of the Secret Service division. Imagine, the president's daughter making out with the hired help—"

"Hired help?" I squeaked, so angry I felt my blood boiling. But Max pressured my foot with his to warn me not to say anything stupid.

He cut to the chase. "What do you want, Brittany? I mean, I assume you want *something* since you've gone through all the trouble of breaking into Morgan's room and stalking us."

"You make it sound so ugly." Brittany pouted.

"Blackmail *is* ugly," he said, stone-cold sober without

an ounce of emotion.

Yikes, Max was a little scary when he got into Secret Service mode. Even soulless Brittany seemed intimidated. But it lasted only a sec. "I want my class presidency back."

"*What?!*" I screeched.

Max frowned warningly at me. "*Morgan*—let's hear her out."

"The presidency in exchange for my . . . discretion. I want you to make the announcement now while the whole class is upstairs."

I was appalled. "But I can't give you back the position. Only AOP's administration can do that."

Brittany airily waved the phone under my nose. "We can sort out the details later. Deal?"

"Max?" I turned to him, hoping for something, anything that could get us out of this mess.

But Max said nothing. His controlled expression meant she worried him more than he was letting on.

My stomach bottomed out. I *knew* she'd pull something like this. I should've been watching her. My fault, my fault, my fault . . .

I heaved a huge sigh. "Agreed."

"Wait a minute—" Max began, but Brittany interrupted him.

"You'd better be convincing when you make the

announcement, Abbott."

"Don't worry." I started to push past her. "I'm a great actress."

Max caught my arm. "You don't have to do this, Morgan."

"Yes I do." I softened when I looked into his blue eyes, full of concern for me. "I want to. Who cares about being class president? It takes up all my free time anyway."

"Morgan—"

"It's okay." I shook him off. "C'mon, Whittaker. Let's go."

In the Yellow Oval Room, the party was still in full swing. The aroma of Mexican chocolate from Nigel's flan filled the air. An embarrassingly large group of girls had trapped Cin'Qua by the thoroughly destroyed buffet table and were begging him to sign autographs on napkin scraps.

Hannah caught sight of me in the doorway. She pulled herself away from Cin'Qua and hurried over. "Where have you been?" she asked. "Everyone's waiting for your speech. . . ." Her voice trailed off when she saw Brittany behind me.

"It's okay, Hans. I'm ready to make my speech now."

I headed out to the balcony and made my way onto the mini stage. Luckily no one had cut the sound to the microphone yet. "Attention! Hey, everyone! I have an announcement to make."

My classmates filed out onto the balcony.

"Let's give it up to Morgan for saving our senior class," Carl yelled, and began clapping and hollering. Whoops filled the air.

Wow. It felt so great to be appreciated by my peers like that. This must've been how Mom felt giving her acceptance speech—minus the feeling of impending doom from a blackmail threat, of course.

They cheered for so long, I had to hold up my hands. Finally, Jeong's whistle cut over the noise. "Let her speak," he yelled. "Go on, Class President."

"Thank you all for coming," I began. Then the reality of what I was about to say caught up with me. I swallowed hard. "It's been a true honor to be your class president, even if it was only for a short time."

Everyone got really quiet.

"What are you talking about, Morgan?" Carl demanded.

"I've decided to relinquish my presidency. The, um, time commitment is too, uh, much for me. I need to concentrate, um, on getting my grades up. Therefore, Brittany Whittaker will assume the office."

Gasps. I caught sight of Mom's shocked face.

Brittany floated gracefully up to the stage and stood modestly to the side. Tears threatened, but I kept it together. "I believe Brittany will be a good steward of our class resources—"

"She almost screwed us out of our graduation party," someone yelled into the shocked silence.

"—and I hope everyone will support her. Thank you."

I stepped down. Brittany stopped me. "You should have asked me to say a few words," she hissed.

"Knock yourself out."

The deafening quiet was starting to dissipate, and an angry murmur was morphing into a full-on roar. Brittany's expression became uneasy. "You'd better say something to calm everyone down."

"You're the class president now, Brits."

I kept my head held high as I walked out of the Yellow Oval Room and down the hallway to the West Sitting Hall. I needed a minute to mellow out and gather myself together. I didn't want to start bawling in front of everyone.

I stared out the Tiffany half-moon window at the end of the room. I took a few deep gulps of air. Giving up my presidency to Brittany Whittaker not once but twice sucked.

But losing Max would suck more.

No contest.

"Morgan, what's going on?"

I turned. Hannah had followed me, as I knew she would. "You can't give your presidency back to Brit the

71

Twit," she said. "She's already screwed everything up once. Prom and graduation will be horrible with her in charge."

"Long story, Hans."

"I've got time."

I explained about Brittany's blackmail. "What else could I do?"

"You could have decked her," Hannah said darkly.

"Then she would have sued me *and* published the photo. No, this was the best way. This party did take a lot of time and at least I'm leaving the senior bank account flush."

"What about the rest of the year? You've made a big difference in a short amount of time. Folks are going to be majorly pissed off at you for walking away from the office and letting Brittany mess everything up all over again."

"I thought you were supposed to make me feel better."

Hannah wrapped me in a tight hug. I ignored her bangles pressing into me and hugged her back. Hard.

"Someday you're going to have to stand up to her," she said. "You can't let her control you."

"If it was only me, I would. But her blackmail affects Max, too. I can't risk it."

The fiery light in Hannah's eyes dimmed. "I guess not."

I took a deep breath. "Guess we'd better get back. This is still my party."

In the Yellow Oval Room, most of the guests had already left. Brittany Whittaker equaled major buzzkill.

Mom and Dad were chatting with Humberto and Cin'Qua. Mom caught sight of me and hurried over. "Everything okay, sweetie?"

"I'll be fine."

"What's this business about you giving up your presidency?"

"I, uh, wanted to get my grades up."

"But—"

"Sara, I think you should drop it." Dad had come up and put a hand on my mom's shoulder. "We need to respect Morgan's decisions."

"But—"

"Why don't you finish saying good-bye to the rest of the guests, Puddin' Pop?" Dad suggested firmly.

I took his hint to escape before my mom weaseled the real reason out of me.

While I was saying good-bye to the remaining guests, Brittany approached me. She had wrapped a butter-yellow pashmina around her bony shoulders.

"A very satisfactory evening, Morgan." Brittany snuggled into her wrap. "Loved the big surprise at the end."

"Glad you had a good time," I said tonelessly. "Now that you have what you want, give me what I want. Delete the photo from your cell phone right now."

"I don't think so."

"What do you mean? You have your presidency back. What more do you want from me?"

"Well, that's just it. The possibilities are endless."

She leaned into me and whispered, "I'll let you know when I need another favor."

That's why my mom didn't negotiate with terrorists. Once you give in you never stop giving.

Chapter Ten

The weather turned nippy and the trees along the Tidal Basin sported the gorgeous autumn colors of late October. Fall break loomed right around the corner, and with it, the upcoming trip to London. Thank god, because Brittany Whittaker was working overtime to wear out my last nerve.

Since the disastrous evening when she blackmailed me into giving up my class presidency, she'd become a mini despot over me. I dealt with her outrageous demands the best I could. Letting her cut in front of me in the lunch line, fine. Allowing her spoiled baby cousin to bowl in the White House bowling alley, no prob. Season tickets to the "President's Own" band concerts for her grandparents, sure thing. About the only thing she didn't do was ask to copy my homework—which, if we were honest, had taken a turn southward since I'd gotten so stressed out about her maniacal control over me. I regretted ever wasting an ounce of sympathy on her.

She'd gotten so bad about squeezing me for favors, I stopped telling Max about them. I knew it would make him angry, and there was nothing he could do . . . well, except tap her phone or freeze her bank account or some other Secret Service mojo that still wouldn't solve my problem. Brittany had evidence that a Secret Service agent was dating the First Daughter, which would either end Max's career or get him shipped off to Timbuktu. I could live with Brittany's tyranny. I couldn't live without Max.

After chem class, I walked to my locker. Hannah was pulling out her civics book for next period. She took one look at my face. "What does Brits want now?"

"She wants me to ask my mom if she can have a ride on Marine One. I'm like, *are you serious*? You want me to bug my mom—the freaking president of the United States—so you can take a helicopter ride and land on the White House lawn?"

Hannah shook her head. "You gotta do something about her, Morg."

"Yeah, but what? I can't risk her blabbing about Max and me to the gossip columns. Mom's having a hard enough time as it is keeping the press off my back." I slammed the door to my locker.

"Have the CIA kidnap her and put her in some cy-ops brainwashing program. Implant someone else's memories in her head. Maybe then she'd turn into, like, *a human being* instead of a snake?"

"I like the way you think." I sighed. "I'll figure out some way to deal with her. She can't keep being a bitch forever."

"I dunno, hasn't she been one since we've known her?"

Hannah had a point. Brits's bitch factor was legendary and showed no signs of stopping.

After school, per the plan, I met Max in the White House basement near the boiler room. I'd been dreaming about being in his arms practically all day, another reason why my grade point average was trending lower. I couldn't stop thinking about him!

As soon as he wrapped his arms around me, I melted. Seriously. Just melted.

"C'mere, you," he murmured.

After a long moment of sheer bliss, he pulled away. "Something bothering you? You seem . . . distracted."

Wow, Max was good. But I didn't want to waste valuable Max time talking about Brittany.

"I'm bummed that I'll be in London for a whole week without you. Can't you get assigned to the security entourage?"

Max let loose a genuine grin, the kind that never failed

to knock my socks off. "How 'bout I do one better and meet you in London?"

"Max! For reals?"

"Yeah. For reals." I flipped out and hugged him super-hard. Max struggled for air.

"We're sure to have more breathing room in another country," I said. "The press won't be on my case twenty-four-seven like they are here."

"Morgan—"

"We can have more alone time!"

"Uh . . ."

"Maybe we can see a play in the West End or hit a club in Piccadilly Circus!" Excitement vroomed through me. Finally, quality alone time with Max!

He grabbed my shoulders. "Morgan, listen. I'm not going to have as much time as I'd like to spend with you in London."

"What? Why?"

"I've got some business to take care of."

"What sort of business?"

He hesitated.

"Come on, Max. We're not supposed to keep secrets. Okay, scratch that. We're not supposed to keep secrets from *each other*. I'm your girlfriend, remember?" Eep. *Girlfriend*. How did that slip out?

"Yeah. You're my girlfriend." A look of wonder crossed his face. Mine, too. It felt really good to say the words—and hear them. "All right, then. I've been approached by the SIS."

"What's that?"

"Secret Intelligence Service. MI6 division."

"Still clued out, Max."

"Britain's covert intelligence organization."

"Oh, like the CIA, but British style?"

He nodded, serious now. "I can't share the particulars, but we're in discussions to set up a global program of agents who skew to a younger demographic. Ones who can infiltrate certain places and mesh with the surroundings more efficiently."

"I get it. Like you meshing in at AOP. Except it'll be . . ." I trailed off as it hit me.

"In London."

The silence between us grew.

"I might not get the job," he said. "I've never really had to interview before."

"Don't worry about that," I said dully. "You'll do great."

"You think so?" He perked up. "It sounds stupid, but I've always wanted to be a real James Bond. Except with less blood and explosions."

"And scantily clad women hanging all over you."

"It's a tough job," he quipped.

I laughed because his eyes were begging me to, but it sounded weak. If Max got the MI6 assignment, he could be sent anywhere around the world. The Middle East. Africa. My mind closed off at the scenarios forming in my head.

The separations could tear us apart.

"Hey, let's not get ahead of ourselves." He gathered me close again. "It's just an interview."

"Yeah." I toyed with a button on his shirt absent-mindedly.

"Plus, you'll be going off to college soon. We'll have to get used to being apart anyway."

"Not if I don't pass my classes at AOP. I'm definitely skirting the two-point-oh GPA line." I tried to sound casual and failed miserably.

His hug tightened. "You'll get your grades up. You always do."

"This time I'm not so sure. God, Max, I don't know if I want to go to college anyway."

"Really?" His arms loosened enough to allow him to look down at me, surprised.

"First off, I have no idea what I want to do with my life. I can't see wasting four years and all that money if I'm going to flunk out."

"Flunk out? You won't flunk out. Not a chance."

How could he understand? He probably finished college in two months. "College is much harder than high school, and I'm already struggling. Plus everyone's bugging me to hurry up and apply to a bunch of schools and pick a major, and basically decide my entire life. Honestly, I don't know what to do."

"Hey, hey, relax." He cupped my face. "You don't have to figure everything out right now. Give it time. The answer will come to you. You've got so much going for you. *Of course* everyone wants to help you make these decisions. Because you're awesome."

"Aww." I got a little misty. Max was so sweet.

"And don't stress about the trip. We'll find some alone time in London," he continued, bending his head closer to mine. "Nothing keeps 007 from romancing a beautiful woman."

Chapter Eleven

"Morg, you weren't kidding when you said I'd be blinded by the light. Those photographers took a million snaps a second." Hannah plopped down into a leather bucket seat and managed to look cool as a cucumber in a leopard print dress topped with a leather jacket. We'd just boarded Air Force One, and the crush of press on the tarmac to see the First Family off on our United Kingdom trip had been intense.

"I warned you." I'd decided on a pair of wide-legged slacks and a cute cutaway jacket for the photo op. The Office of Protocol had briefed us on the amount of media scrutiny we'd receive. Rumors that Prince Richard and I were an item had persisted since his visit to D.C. last month, and the gossip rags were in full swing. Luckily for Hannah, they didn't know the truth. For me, it became a real PITA—Pain in the Ass.

Hannah had barely sat down when she whipped out her cell phone and started hitting the buttons.

"Texting Prince Richard again?" I teased.

"You know it. He's at Balmoral right now, but he's 'motoring down' and we'll meet up tomorrow. *Motoring down* . . . isn't that so cute and Britishy?" She sighed dreamily at the tiny keypad in her hand.

Yep, she had it bad.

We settled into the airplane stateroom reserved for the president's immediate family. The head steward offered Hannah and me the movie menu while he fixed us a snack. George was hanging with the Secret Service posse in their midcabin cubby. Mom was in the Executive Suite, a private room within the airplane's stateroom, confabbing with Humberto and a slew of State Department diplomats. Mom was hoping this trip, which came on the heels of her major success negotiating a nonproliferation treaty with the renegade African juntas last month, would solidify her international reputation as a key world leader. Though she'd never let on, I could tell she had a lot riding on this trip. Hopefully, I wouldn't add to her worries by messing anything up.

Hannah and I were still deciding which movie to watch when out on the tarmac, photographers and camera crews started going nuts again.

"What the—?" I couldn't believe my eyes. Out of the porthole window, Brittany Whittaker was sashaying up the gangplank and into the plane, followed by her dad, Senator Whittaker.

At the same moment, my mother emerged from her office in the Executive Suite. "I know, I know." She held up her hand placatingly when she saw the thunder brewing on my face. "I don't want the Whittakers with us, either."

"But, *Mom!*" I wailed.

"It's a political decision to bring Senator Whittaker to London. We're working on a bipartisan solution to the international nuclear proliferation treaties. I need him on the negotiation team. At the last minute he asked if he could bring Brittany along since her plans to spend fall break with her mother in Barbados fell through."

"Wonder why," Hannah muttered.

The door to the stateroom cabin opened, and Parker poked his head in. "Senator Whittaker's arrived," he said.

"Ask Chet and his daughter to come in."

"Can't you make them sit in the Press Pool?" I hissed. The Press Pool in the back of the plane was notoriously cramped and somewhat stinky as the plane lavatories were located back there.

"Don't think I didn't consider it," Mom quipped. Then she composed herself, a "presidential" expression on her face. "Chet, welcome aboard."

Chet Whittaker entered the stateroom, followed by Brittany wearing a megaload of foundation and eyeliner.

"Thank you, Madam President." Senator Whittaker put his arm around Brittany. "Our apologies for being late. We had a last-minute emergency, didn't we, sugar?"

"Our housekeeper let the dog out." Brittany sniffed. "Moron."

"Uh, darlin', why don't you settle in here with the girls?" Mr. Whittaker said hurriedly. "We don't want to hold the president up any longer, do we?"

"My aides tell me we're still on schedule," Mom replied. "Morgan, maybe Brittany would like to watch the movie with you and Hannah."

I glared at Mom and she winced. Hannah looked like she wanted to hurt someone.

"You'd like that, wouldn't you, hon?" Senator Whittaker gave Brittany's shoulder a pat.

Brittany looked about as excited as Hannah and I felt. "I guess I have no choice."

"Then it's settled," Mom said brightly. "Have fun, girls." She stepped back into her office with Chet Whittaker right on her heels.

Oh, she'd *so* be making this up to me later.

We prepared for takeoff. As we were taxiing down the

runway, Hannah leaned over to Brittany. "Morgan has to be nice to you. But I don't. Ya get what I'm saying, Brits?"

"*Pfft*. You don't scare me, Davis. And if you piss me off, Morgan will pay the price."

She had us there. Hannah sank back in her seat.

Nine hours stuck on a plane with Brittany Whittaker was a total nightmare. If she wasn't complaining about the food from the airplane galley, she was forcing us to watch the shlock horror flicks she liked. I almost cried when I learned she and her dad were staying at the same hotel as us due to the high level of security needed for the presidential entourage, which included her father, as Brittany loved to repeat ad nauseam. Hannah and I finally had to pretend to sleep to get her to shut up about it.

Air Force One touched down on Gatwick's private runway at dawn. My eyelids felt gummy and my mouth ashy. Even Hannah, always the picture of perfection, looked droopy, and her expression was dull. I could hear staff members, press, and Secret Service agents stirring and moaning about cramped muscles. Only Brittany seemed to have no problem getting enough sleep; she snuffled in the seat next to me with her eyes swathed in a black eye mask.

Hannah now had to travel to the hotel with Brittany, her father, and the rest of Mom's staff, darkening her mood further. From the airport, Mom and I were headed straight to 10 Downing Street, the prime minister's residence.

In the unmarked U.K. government limo, Mom looked fresh and rested even after a night of airplane travel. "How'd the flight go with Brittany?" she asked.

"Nightmare" was about all I wanted to say on the subject.

Mom laughed ruefully. "Well, I owe you one. I never would have suggested that Chet bring Brittany on our trip knowing how you feel about her. But—"

"You need to keep the opposition happy," I finished.

Mom nodded. "Politics," she said. "There are thousands of pieces moving in this game of international chess. The upcoming G-Eight summit, the new nuclear nonproliferation treaty . . . I need them all to fit, and unfortunately, Chet Whittaker is one of my rooks."

"It's okay, Mom. If you can deal with having a Whittaker around, so can I." Or so I hoped. As long as Brittany didn't find out about Max meeting me in London.

I forgot about Brittany when we hit the M25 motorway leading to London, and the motorcade lengthened. Every so often, cheery homemade signs with the words WELCOME, PRESIDENT ABBOTT or WE LOVE YOU, MORGAN! whizzed by. There were also a few MAKE TEA NOT WAR signs, which made me giggle.

Since the Secret Service and MI6 had decided that a full-blown entrance into London wouldn't be wise considering the recent spate of terrorist threats, our motorcade took an unpublicized route to Westminster. Glitzy modern buildings marched side by side with old Victorian brick row houses. Pubs dotted every corner, and I was excited to see London Underground portals. I hoped I could ride the Tube just once while I was here, if I could talk George into allowing it. "Look, a red telephone booth!"

A tall, red, rectangular kiosk with a crown and the word TELEPHONE whipped by.

"God, this place is cool." I wanted to stop the motorcade, get out, run to the nearest pub, and order fish and chips.

"It really is," Mom said. She had this peaceful look on her face, the one she wore whenever she traveled. Mom had come from a family of famous diplomats, and she'd never lost the travel bug. "I can't wait to show you some of my old haunts."

"Cool."

We pulled into an underground garage, which would lead us to a secret entry into the home of the British prime minister, Owen Eckley. Humberto had already gone ahead with the advance team and was waiting for us. After giving us a moment to catch our breath, Humberto checked his watch. "It's time."

We were ushered into an elevator, which had been reinforced with bulletproof steel.

Mom smoothed her bob, though it was already perfect. "How do I look?" she asked.

She wore a conservative blue suit with a tiny entwined Union Jack/Stars and Stripes flag pin on her lapel. Minimal makeup, natural lip gloss, and yet power radiated from her.

"Presidential," I said.

Then the elevator doors opened.

Chapter Twelve

As soon as the doors parted, a camera flash went off right in my face.

"Got her," I heard a British voice say before a round of applause drowned it out.

We'd come straight into what I supposed was the foyer of 10 Downing Street. Diplomats and dignitaries packed the space, but after I blinked out the black dots swimming before my eyes, I saw no journalists or camera crews as per protocol. The press op was scheduled for later, in front of Number 10's famous front door, after the official meet and greet.

So . . . who had taken the photo?

A man stepped out of the crowd toward Mom—Owen Eckley, the prime minister. His thinning hair didn't do his freckled skull any favors, but he beamed at us with his famous smile, which could be either charming or sharkish, depending on the mood or moment. We were in charm-mode now. "Welcome to London, Madam President."

Mom clasped his hands and said some formal words of thanks. I tuned out the Official Diplomatic Pleasantries phase. Bitter experience had taught me that it would be long-winded and boring in the extreme. It was.

"And this must be your lovely daughter, Morgan." Prime Minister Eckley turned his attention to me. Toothy grin. "Good lord. She looks just like you."

"It's been noted once or twice," Mom answered drily.

"No, really. She looks *exactly* like you—"

"These must be your sons," Mom interjected.

"Ahem, yes." Prime Minister Eckley motioned for four boys, who'd inherited their father's white-blond hair and freckles, to step forward. I'd already been briefed on each, but I nodded politely to them as their father introduced them. "Alban, my eldest, he's at Cambridge now studying global economics; Trevor, finishing his last year at public school, has just finished his A levels—"

"Haa-low there," Trevor drawled. White lashes rimmed his brown eyes, giving them a skeevy reptilian vibe.

Trevor's lizard eyes drifted over me, focusing a little too long on my boobs. Then I noticed the digital camera in his hands. "How about another picture?" He draped one arm around my shoulder, positioned the camera with his other, and snapped another shot. Based on the angle of the camera, I'm not sure my head was in the frame.

Ugh. Down, boy.

The prime minister gave Trevor a disapproving look, and just like that Trevor backed away. "And these are Callum and Rhys, my twins."

More pleasantries, and somehow the prime minister's chief of staff got us moved into a drawing room distinguished by two massive pillars, a Persian carpet, and a portrait of some queen over a fancy fireplace.

Blah blah, the pleasantries kept coming. I wondered if we were going to get something to eat soon. I was starved. I was zoned out thinking about fruit scones with clotted cream and other British fare that Nigel would have served up had he been in charge of the meal when I felt a pulse of hot air on my neck. I looked over my shoulder.

Trevor Eckley was *right there*, breathing on me.

I moved away, pointedly.

"I know it's not on the agenda, but I'd like to work in a discussion of expanding the women's microloan program to the developing nations," Mom was saying to the PM. "The initiative is doing well in the U.S. and I think its international deployment is timely, given the global economic situation at present."

Eckley pursed his lips and looked thoughtful. "But

does this little 'women's issue' bear discussion now, when we have other pressing matters on the agenda?"

"Women's issue?"

I thought only I caught the tension in Mom's voice, but maybe the PM picked up on her mood, too, because suddenly his grin flashed and he turned to me. "And how is Morgan finding London?"

Got it. The ol' redirect-the-conversation-to-the-kids routine to dodge the issue. For the sake of Anglo-American relations, I played along. "What little I've seen looks lovely," I said politely.

"Perhaps my son Trevor could be your escort for your stay? He knows London and what the kids are up to these days with the new music scene and so forth."

What? No. Dear god, no.

Before I could say anything, Trevor chipped in. "Love to, Dad. I've got a few . . . things I could show her."

Kill. Me. Now.

"Thanks, but I've got my visit pretty well covered," I said. "Security issues, you know—"

The PM waved his hand. "We can take care of all that. Trevor will liven things up for you, don't worry."

"I'll give you the insiders' London tour," Trevor said. Skeevy leer.

Could the guy be any grosser?

I threw Mom a pleading look. She bit her lip and I could tell she was trying to decide what was worse: offending the Eckleys or suffering my wrath.

My wrath lost.

"It shouldn't be a problem for the Secret Service to rearrange the agenda," she said. "We do it all the time."

My mom had just thrown me under the bus—a red double-decker bus.

"Excellent!" Prime Minister Eckley beamed. "We'll let them make their plans without parental interference, eh, Sara?"

"You'll have the time of your life." Trevor's lizard eyes swept over me. "Guaranteed."

Mercifully, one of Prime Minister Eckley's aides whispered that our press conference on the front steps of Number 10 was ready to roll, ending the unpleasant discussion.

With George shadowing my left shoulder and Parker's team circling Mom in a protective bubble, we headed outside. The cheers from the throng pressed against the police barricades deafened me. British police in their bobby hats held clubs at their waists to ensure no one broke through security. Then the Secret Service agents stepped away from us, and the media immediately started firing off shots while camera crews and reporters rushed to the front.

It was all a bit insane, but I'd seen worse. At least everyone in Britain was shoving politely.

Mom fielded a few questions about the upcoming G8 preparation talks and one about her recent success negotiating a cease-fire in Africa, which had prevented a rogue nation from selling yellowcake uranium to terrorists.

"Morgan!" one of the journalists screamed. "Morgan, who are you wearing?"

I looked down at my outfit. Hannah had spiffed up one of the dreary pantsuits. "I'm not sure," I said. "But I'll bet it was made in America."

Chuckles rippled through the crowd.

"Where are the colored hair extensions?" another called.

"I . . . uh, decided I was ready for a new look." When I had to impersonate my mother last month.

"Any news on your love life?"

"Just that there's no news."

More laughter, camera strobes going off. Man, these paparazzi were aggressive.

"What are your plans after high school, Morgan? Have you chosen a college yet?"

"Well, I . . . uh . . . there's so much to think about. . . . "

"Would you consider Oxford or Cambridge?"

Yikes, Oxford or Cambridge wouldn't consider *me* once they looked at my transcript.

It didn't happen often, but I was at a loss for words. Fortunately, Mom stepped in. "It's wonderful that young women these days have so many options open to them. I hope that someday women all over the globe will have the same opportunities that we do in our countries. Thank you!"

Mom waved. She nudged me and I waved, too. Then the Secret Service team closed in and we were swallowed back up into Number 10.

Trevor Eckley was on the other side of the door. "You and your mother are quite the team, aren't you? That's one way to ensure a women's issue makes it on the front pages."

"Got a problem with that?" I said.

"Oh no." Trevor gave me an oilier version of his dad's grin. "I like a girl who's clever."

Since I didn't really care about Trevor Eckley's likes or dislikes, especially after that crack about "women's issues," I shrugged without answering and put some space between us. I didn't want to cause an international incident by blowing up at the PM's son within hours of stepping on British soil.

When I looked back, he was still smiling at me goofily. How was I going to ditch him and Brittany and spend time with Max? So far my trip to London was—as the British say—a bloody nightmare.

Chapter Thirteen

"I can't believe you're already up," I said, rubbing my eyes and trying to remember where in space and time I was. With the jet lag and the exhausting political mumbo jumbo, I'd come back to the hotel and crashed.

"Fabulousness takes time." Hannah peered into the full-length mirror and rearranged a stray corkscrew strand in her carefully wild hairdo. "I want Rich's jaw to drop when he sees me."

"The prince is going to pass out," I said, admiring her body-hugging skinny jeans and boho-chic jacket. Hannah looked stellar when she wasn't half trying.

I sat up in bed and pushed my rat's-nest hair out of my face. Gray early-morning light filtered through the curtain sheers. Though our hotel suite was situated on the top floor, I could still hear the faint grumble of London traffic below.

"Rich is whisking me away on the royals' helicopter for my first day in England," Hannah remarked. "He wants to give me a private tour."

"Wow!"

"Do you and Max want to come along?"

"I can't." Arg, it hurt to say that, because I'd love nothing more than to fly over the beautiful English countryside with my peeps. "Max is busy, and I promised Mom I'd spend the day with her. We have an exciting international roundtable on global green energy to attend first thing this morning. Fun times!"

"Blerg. Hey, maybe tonight we can hook up and go to the theater?"

"Love it! I'll talk to George about security. Let's make it happen!"

Cheered, I watched Hannah try on several different configurations of hoop earrings while I threw on a conservative pair of black slacks, a pointy-collared shirt, and flats. After polishing off a traditional English breakfast of bacon, sausage, eggs, grilled mushrooms, and toast—weirdly delicious topped with baked beans—and milky, sweet, hot tea, I wondered how Americans were the most obese nation if the British ate this much every morning. I felt a bit carbo-sluggish. I told George that I was ready whenever Mom wanted to head out.

Normally I hated the whole First Daughter routine. Not only did I have to keep a lid on what I said and did because of the intense media scrutiny, but there was a 95 percent chance I'd mess something up and land on the "Oh No She Didn't!" section of the gossip columns. But Mom seemed so psyched about giving me greater insights into the shark tank known as world politics, I couldn't disappoint her.

So Hannah got a helicopter ride with a gorgeous prince; I got stuck in meetings with super-serious politicians. I tried not to be jealous because I was happy for Hannah . . . but it was hard.

A knock came at the door. "It's probably George," I yelled to Hannah, who'd commandeered our spacious bathroom and was now delicately touching up her mascara. "I'll get it."

And there *she* was. Brittany Whittaker and about three pounds of floral perfume clouding the air. She slinked past me while I stood frozen in stunned surprise. "You're both awake, I see. Somehow I didn't take you for an early bird, Abbott." Her eyes swept Hannah, who'd popped out of the bathroom when she heard Brittany's voice. "And the two of you are all dressed up. What's going on today?"

"None of your business," Hannah said aggressively. "I already had to put up with your whining last night, Whittaker." Hannah pulled an exaggerated bitch face and mimicked, "'Ew, Daddy, London smells like a toilet; Daddy, I want to stop at Harrods right now.' I'm not in the mood for your b.s. today."

"Easy there, Davis. I'm trying to be friendly. Americans abroad together and all that. I thought we could hang out. I'm bored."

Hang out? With Brittany Whittaker?

Hannah and I exchanged appalled glances. The last thing Hannah needed was Brittany finding out that she and Prince Richard were hooking up. One threat of blackmail between the two of us was enough.

"This isn't *Sisterhood of the Traveling Pants*." Hannah decided on the direct route. "So buzz off and find someone else's day to ruin."

"PMS-ing much, Davis? Morgan, are you going to let her be so mean to me?"

"Let me think." I pressed a finger to my lips as if contemplating world peace. "Uh, yeah."

Brittany shrugged. She reached into her handbag overloaded with tons of buckles and unearthed her cell phone. "I guess I'll have to send this photo of you and Max to my contact at *The Gadfly* after all. If we're going to be mean to each other, that is."

"That's *it*!" Anger erupted out of me. "I am so *sick* of your blackmail!" I lunged toward her.

"Hey!"

I swung at the phone in Brittany's hand. It sailed through the air and landed safely on my unmade bed, where I snatched it up and flicked it open.

"Oh my god," I breathed. "You don't even have service."

Now I remembered! George told me our mobile service would be disabled while we were in London because of security concerns. The Secret Service must have disabled the wireless capabilities of everyone attached to the president's entourage.

Brittany wouldn't be able to use her cell phone at all while she was in the U.K.—glory hallelujah and God save the queen!

She clawed at the phone. "Give me my phone back, or I'll . . . I'll tell my father."

"Go for it. And I'll tell him what a conniving snake you are."

"Well, I'll tell your mother that you're sleazing around with your Secret Service agent— Where are you going?"

I flicked my head toward Hannah in a signal to sneak out before I marched toward the bathroom. "I'm going to find out how well your cell phone works after British toilet water has soaked its circuits."

Hannah clapped a hand over her mouth to stifle a laugh and edged out of the room.

Now Brittany freaked. Moving faster than I could imagine on her spiky heels, she pinned me against the doorjamb. "Give. It. Back."

"Make me," I said, my inner four-year-old shining through.

She snatched at the phone. We arm-wrestled for a few breathless seconds until her talons viciously dug into my wrist. I yelped and my fingers loosened.

"Yes!" She pried the cell phone away and clutched it protectively to her chest, tottering to the door. "As soon as I get back to the U.S., I'm sending this photo to every major press outlet I can find. You and your boyfriend are on borrowed time, Abbott."

She slammed the door behind her.

I blew out a long breath. That was intense.

I knew there'd be a price to pay for getting into it with Brittany. But maybe it wouldn't matter in the long run if Max got the job with MI6.

I plopped down on the rumpled bed and absently rubbed the moon-shaped welts Brittany's claws had left on my wrist. I thought about Max. I wanted the best for him; I truly did. Working for MI6 would be a dream come true for him . . . but I couldn't pretend that things hadn't been strained between us. Between getting ready for the trip and his responsibilities with the Secret Service, we hadn't been able to spend much time together. And now with the newly fired-up Brittany, I needed to watch my back more closely than ever. She'd love to get more dirt on us to feed to the U.S. press.

I toyed with calling Max to wish him good luck on his interview today. But then I'd have to use the landline, which was monitored by security. I couldn't risk it.

Another knock on the door. Brittany, coming back for round two?

I yanked it open. "I'm not in the mood for any more of your bullsh—oh. Hi, George."

The elf-brows on George's face shot up to her hairline. "I haven't given you any b.s. yet, Morgan."

"I thought you were someone else."

"Obviously." She peered into the wrecked room and her brows arched even higher. "Wow, looks like a tornado hit this room."

Tornado. My Secret Service code name.

"I'll try to keep other weather-related disasters to a minimum on this trip, George. I promise."

"I'm not holding my breath," George muttered.

Chapter Fourteen

Mom and I took an unmarked car to the Houses of Parliament to meet Prime Minister Eckley for the first round of Anglo-American forums. Parliament's Gothic spires stabbed the murky gray morning sky. I'd seen my share of majestic architecture, but when the motorcade rolled past Westminster Abbey I was blown away. Sure, we Americans could be proud of our historical monuments, but the Brits had that centuries-old thing going on, so advantage Brittania.

"Gorgeous, isn't it?" Mom had donned a houndstooth blazer over a pair of tan slacks. She'd been up all night reading EU economic-recovery plans but looked fresh and ready to go. I, however, was still jet-laggy, carbo-loaded, and annoyed over my altercation with Brittany. "The city of London is amazing."

"It sure is." I couldn't wait to explore the trendy shops,

happening hot spots, and more of that traditional British cuisine. I hoped I could ditch the meetings later so I could do just that.

The car swung into the New Palace Yard, swarming with Secret Service and MI6 security. Tourists and Londoners gawked as George and Parker quickly bundled us out of the car and through the Member's Entrance.

My jaw dropped once we were escorted into the Central Lobby. Intricate paneling inset with life-size carvings of medieval kings and queens lined the octagonal room. A stunning display of windows with tiny window panes soared up to a cone-shaped spire, which threw light down on red, white, and blue ceramic tiles on the floor painted with medieval stuff like British lions and heraldic symbols.

Prime Minister Owen Eckley and his toothy grin greeted us in front of a life-size statue of William Gladstone. "Welcome to Westminster, President Abbott. Morgan." Genially he shook Mom's hand, then mine.

"President Abbott." Trevor Eckley bounded out from behind his father and wrung Mom's hand.

Trevor? What the heck?

"I thought it was a brilliant idea bringing your daughter along to spend the day immersing in international politics," Owen Eckley told Mom after they exchanged greetings under a fusillade of snapping cell phone cameras from onlookers and low-level staff members. "So brilliant, in fact, I've brought along Trevor for the same experience."

Trevor smiled smarmily at me, and his weird eyes swiped my boobs again.

"I thought my son could keep Morgan company if our discussions on international climate treaties got too dull for her," Prime Minister Eckley continued. "Maybe Trevor could take her on a tour of Portcullis House and Big Ben, properly accompanied by Morgan's security team, of course."

Oh yeah, George would love an unauthorized trip to a tourist site without sweeping it eighty million times for security threats. I was gagging over the thought of spending the afternoon with Trevor Eckley.

"I'm sure we can find something to do," Trevor said.

Barf.

"I'll let Morgan decide when she's ready," Mom said, reading my pleading face not to throw me to the Trevor-wolf. "Shall we get started? We have a full agenda today."

Now I'm all about restricting greenhouse emissions and saving the polar bears and keeping the Arctic Circle from melting into the sea. But listening to a room full of scientists and politicians—especially that windbag Senator Whittaker—discuss the best way to enforce a worldwide climate treaty made me wish I'd taken some NoDoz beforehand.

Seriously, the discussions were so boring and the speeches so long-winded, I wondered how Mom was able to maintain her alert expression, especially when the talk centered on how low-carbon–growth jobs could lead to more economic recovery in developing nations. But no one could settle on a clear formula for determining the growth. The debate went on and on and on. Even George, normally so stoic, couldn't stop her eyes from glazing over. Trevor sat next to me texting like a maniac on his mobile, which only reminded me that I'd been deprived of my main means of communication. Otherwise I'd have texted Max to find out how his interview had gone.

Max. I missed him so much.

I felt a hand slide along mine. *Ready to get out of here?* Trevor mouthed.

I jerked away. Luckily I was spared telling him to back off because the meeting suddenly broke up. Senator Whittaker snapped his fingers at one of his aides to gather a mountain of papers that had been handed out at the meeting, while the rest of the presidential entourage unkinked their necks and stretched.

"Still awake?" Mom said to me with a chuckle. "These meetings can take forever, but once you get past the posturing, we get good work done."

"What did you kids think of the discussion?" Owen Eckley asked.

I opened my mouth, but Trevor cut me off. "We should hit uncooperative countries with economic sanctions. Serves them right for not playing ball. You're either with us, or you're out. Right, Morgan?" Trevor nudged me conspiratorially in the ribs.

"Erm, interesting line of thinking, son," Prime Minister Eckley said diplomatically. "Morgan? Your thoughts?"

My thoughts?

"Well, the main sticking point seems to be how to get developing countries to switch from high-carbon–producing jobs to low-emission jobs, or green technology. Right?"

Mom nodded. "That's right."

"So instead of focusing on forcing countries to adopt low-carbon–growth jobs in specific areas, why not ask them to agree on an overall percentage? That way they could decide which segments of their economy they want to change. People like to be in control of their own lives, not told what to do by outsiders. The administrators at AOP—"

"AOP?" Prime Minister Eckley queried.

"Morgan's school," Mom said.

"Yeah, the administrators at AOP tell the student council what needs to be done, but they let us figure out how to make it happen," I went on. "Under supervision, of course. It works out well."

"Interesting," the prime minister murmured.

Mom beamed. "That's a very good point, sweetie."

"Plus it'll be easier to agree on a percentage than entire economic policies," I said. "You could cut out about three days of boring and endless meetings, I bet. The House of Parliament is gorgeous and all that, but no one likes to be stuck inside at a snore fest if they can help it."

No one said anything. Trevor Eckley stared at me like I was some sort of alien creature, and his father's mouth sagged open. Even Mom looked surprised.

Oh crap. Tornado and her big mouth had struck again.

Chapter Fifteen

Prime Minister Eckley started to laugh. "No one can accuse your daughter of beating around the bush, Sara. Is she always so forthright?"

"To a fault," Mom said wryly.

"It's refreshing to hear such straight talk, and from someone so young. Overthinking a problem can be as detrimental as underthinking. Wouldn't you agree?"

Mom eyed Owen Eckley carefully, but she kept her expression neutral. Some political power play was happening between them that I suddenly realized had nothing to do with me.

"Would you excuse Morgan and me for a moment?" Mom said sweetly, and drew me aside.

"Did I mess up?" I asked her anxiously.

"Of course not. I'm proud of your response. You showed them you've got a brain and aren't afraid of speaking your mind. However . . . " Here Mom tugged her ear, a gesture she used when she was finessing the situation. "*Snore fest* might have been a step too far. True, but too far." She kissed me on the top of my head. "Maybe you'd be happier doing something else this afternoon. Perhaps a little sightseeing after all?"

I read between the lines. Mom needed me out of the way before I said something really embarrassing.

"What a fantastic idea, Madam President," Trevor interjected. Didn't the guy understand discretion? Who barged into a private conversation like that? "I'd love to show Morgan what London has to offer." Cue ookey smile.

I hesitated. As much as I wanted to get out of the Parliament's stuffy chambers and see the city, hanging with Trevor Eckley all afternoon was the last thing on my mind. I didn't trust the guy *at all*.

"But if you'd prefer to stay here, I'm sure you'll enjoy the next round of meetings, too, honey. We have an exciting docket of trade agreements to hash out, especially the proposed tariffs on textiles." Mom sealed the deal.

I sighed heavily. "Hoo-kay, Trevor. Let's get out of here."

"Fantastic." Trevor tried to take my arm, but I shook him off.

Owen Eckley smirked. "Don't do anything I wouldn't do, son."

"Wouldn't dream of it, Dad."

Did male piggery swim in the Eckley gene pool?

Out in the foyer, Trevor and I waited for George to confab with her MI6 counterpart, who was Trevor's personal bodyguard. A sizable crowd had gathered outside the gates of the courtyard, tipped off that the president had arrived. I spied paparazzi with their zoom lenses trained on the door. We'd have to do a duck and dash to avoid them.

Outside the gates, digital cameras flashed and people screamed my name. I waved. Out of nowhere, Trevor wrapped his arm around me and he mirrored my smile and wave. I hoped the paparazzi could see my skin crawling. We let the paparazzi get a few shots before I discreetly elbowed him away and George bundled me into the unmarked car.

Trevor patted the seat next to him. "Got your space right here, American girl."

"No thanks." I slid closer to George.

A trace of annoyance flicked across his face, but then his expression grew pompous. "We'll start with the Tower of London—you'll want to see the Crown Jewels—or maybe we should go to Westminster Abbey first. . . . "

"Hold up, Trevor. I want to check out Portobello Market first. I hear it's the coolest flea market in the world."

"A flea market? You want to buy *used* clothing?"

"Vintage, one-of-a-kind clothing," I corrected. Did

Trevor ever remove that stick up his rear end?

"Why don't you ask your American designers to send round some free samples from their warehouses? That's what Mum does. Hasn't paid a penny for clothes ever since the election."

"Because the Abbotts don't abuse the power of our office to score free clothes," I told him icily. "Besides, it'll be fun to explore the funky shops and walk around."

He shrugged. "Run it past your security agent. I don't think she'll allow it."

To my fury, Trevor was right. "Sorry, Morgan, we can't secure the location," George said. "Creating a bubble in an open market would take at least forty-eight hours' advance notice."

Grr!

"Well, what about a ride on an open double-decker bus? Tour the city? That can't be much of a security risk, can it?"

George shook her head. "One word: snipers. Can't risk it."

This "sightseeing tour"—i.e., being stuck in a limo in the courtyard—was really starting to blow. "What about a cream tea in a tea shop?" I asked. "There's no security risk in having a snack, is there?"

The look on George's face said it all. A big, fat N-O.

That hurt. I really wanted to try a cream tea, ever since I'd heard Nigel rave about it.

"They canceled your London tour when you decided to go with your mother this morning. If we'd had more advance notice—" George began apologetically.

"It's okay. I guess we can't bubble the entire city of London just for me."

We pulled out of the courtyard and Trevor directed the driver to motor us around Trafalgar Square and over Tower Bridge, but even those experiences were ruined by London's gridlock traffic and the squad of paparazzi on mopeds following our car. Finally, after witnessing more than one close call between paparazzi and pedestrians, I threw in the towel and instructed the driver to head back to our hotel.

So annoying. The afternoon was a complete bust, and my first full day in London was spent in conference rooms and behind bulletproof glass.

The day couldn't get much worse.

And then . . . it did.

Chapter Sixteen

Even though George and Trevor's MI6 agent had us in a highly sophisticated and ironclad security bubble when we returned to the hotel, Trevor insisted on walking me upstairs to my room.

"It's not necessary," I told him when I got into the chrome-plated elevator. "Really. George would flatten anyone who tried to get near me in a nanosecond."

Trevor chuckled. "Just being polite, Morgan. I wouldn't dream of leaving you in the lobby. It's just not cricket."

I'd had enough of Trevor Eckley to last a lifetime, but it wasn't worth arguing over. "Whatever."

The elevator holding the four of us mercifully slid up the side of the building in about five seconds. In the polished metal of the doors, I could see Trevor leaning toward me, and I pointedly shifted away. What would it take for him to get the message I wasn't interested?

George and Trevor's MI6 agent headed toward the make-shift security station at the end of the hallway while Trevor walked me to the door of my room. "Thanks again for the tour," I said.

"Aren't you going to invite me in?"

"Let's call it a day here. I'm bushed. Jet lag, y'know."

I opened the door to my room a crack. I could see the beds were made, the room had been tidied, and fresh bottles of mineral water had been left on the table. I sighed, ready to kick off my flats and collapse, when I felt hot breath on my cheek.

I turned my head. Trevor Eckley was leaning in, trying to look inside my room.

"Back off." I pushed at him.

"You're so cute when you're getting in a tizzy."

"A tizzy?" The *hell*?

"Angry, Morgan. Angry."

He leaned in again. Oh my god, he was going to kiss me!

I dodged and his mouth ended up on my cheek for a wet and slobbery kiss. Paralyzed with disgust, I couldn't even move when he tried again and planted his lips squarely on mine.

Ugh! I'd been slimed, British style.

"You know you want it," Trevor panted when he pulled away. I think he was going for a sexy voice but was failing miserably. "The merging of two powerful nations . . ."

Oh my god. Trevor Eckley had officially surpassed my ex-boyfriend Konner Tippington as the most clued-out male ever.

"What I want is for you to respect my personal space," I said firmly. He swooped in again. I cringed and dodged his lips. While my head was crooked down, I saw Max standing in the hall in front of an open elevator door. He stared at us with a shocked expression, then he turned right around and disappeared back into the elevator.

"Max! Wait!"

The ding of a closing elevator door was all that answered me.

Trevor, incredibly, was still trying to cop a feel. I elbowed him in the gut and ran to the elevators. Desperately I pounded at the buttons until the doors opened and I leaped inside the empty elevator. Maybe I could catch Max in the lobby and explain this latest Morgan mess. It was a total misunderstanding!

Down in the lobby, hotel employees and aides on my mom's staff flurried about in the dance I've come to know as Here Comes the Commander-in-Chief. No one wants to be caught slacking when the president waltzes in. Max cut efficiently between the scurrying bodies and vanished out the front door.

I clenched my fists. Max!

I was about to run after him, the bubble be damned,

when I felt a tug on my arm. "Morgan? Come on, we don't have much time for, you know, games. My old man is expecting me home before teatime."

"You stupid jerk!" I swung around, blazingly furious at Trevor. The trajectory of my bunched fist was unfortunate, because my bared knuckles landed right on his nose.

"Ow!" he yelled, cupping his face.

"Who the hell do you think you are?" I spat at him.

Trevor Eckley blinked in confusion. His voice was muffled behind his hand. "I'm . . . the prime minister's son. And you're the president's daughter. It's fate. Kismet, or something like that. All the tabloids said we'd hook up when you came to visit."

My god. Was he really that idiotic?

I suddenly realized that people were staring at us. I took a deep breath to keep from giving him a matching bruise on his jaw.

"Trevor, listen carefully. I have no interest in you. None. Nada. Zippo. Zilch. There is no kismet between us. The only reason we're together now is because our parents are world leaders. That's it."

Trevor listened to me intently, taking it all in. "So does that mean we're not going to Chinawhite for cocktails?"

A lost cause.

The elevator doors opened, and George and Trevor's

MI6 agent emerged. A thunderous expression darkened George's pixie face. "You'd better have a good explanation for dashing off the floor like a bat outta hell without informing me of your destination first, Morgan."

I did, only it wouldn't be one that George would accept. "I, um, thought I saw someone I knew."

"Thought you knew? Who?"

My teeth gnawed my lower lip. I was too upset to even think up a convincing fib. "Agent Jackson," I said, giving up.

"As in Agent Max Jackson? Here, in London?"

"He, um, ran out the front doors and I hoped I could catch him." My eyes pleaded with her not to ask any probing questions.

"Excellent. Great. This won't end badly *at all*." She shut her eyes briefly, as if she contemplated having her brain checked for sanity. "Do you want me to go after him?"

"Could you?" I breathed in relief. "That would be so cool of you, George. I swear I'd never cause you any problems ever again."

"Don't make any promises you can't keep." George glanced at her MI6 counterpart, who was politely but firmly reaming Trevor for breaking *his* bubble of security. Trevor's hangdog expression and swollen nose were super satisfying. The iron grip the agent had on Trevor's shoulder while he steered him toward the back exit also pleased me.

"All right, I'll try to find him. But you've got to head straight back to your suite. No delays, detours, or more fistfights. Got it?"

Yay! "Got it. And, thank you."

George nodded curtly before heading out the hotel's front doors.

In the elevator zipping back up to the top floor, a wave of exhaustion swamped me. A delayed reaction to having Max see me in the arms of Trevor Eckley, I supposed, coupled with the fact that George now knew Max was in London. And she must suspect there was something more between me and Max. Things were getting complicated fast, and I'd been in town less than forty-eight hours.

The bell dinged when I reached my floor. I was sooo looking forward to getting out of my boring clothes and into a pair of jeans, when the doors slid apart to reveal Brittany Whittaker.

I wasn't catching any breaks today.

"Hey there, Morgan. Back from touring London?"

I elbowed past her. "I haven't seen much yet," I muttered.

"Oooh, too bad. I just got back from a major splurge session in Mayfair." She held up Stella McCartney and Burberry shopping bags. "My dad gave me his black American Express card and told me to go wild. Hm, you look upset. There isn't any trouble in paradise with Supersecret Agent Man, is there?"

The hollow pit in my stomach grew to the size of a

watermelon. "What are you getting at?"

"It's just that most men don't like sharing their girl-friends with other guys. I saw you flirting with that freckly dude. Was that the prime minister's son?" she asked innocently.

I got right in her face. "Careful, Brits. You overplay your hand with me, and you'll get more than you bargained for. Now leave me *and* Max alone."

I stomped off, ignoring her sputters. It felt good to tell Brittany off, but the satisfaction only lasted a second. I knew I'd just given her more ammunition to send that photo of me and Max when we got back to the States. Plus it killed me that Max might have gotten the wrong idea about Trevor. He already felt insecure about dating the president's daughter. I didn't want to give him another reason to question our relationship.

I prayed that George would find him quickly so I could clear the air with him. Maybe we'd even laugh about it later.

Maybe.

Chapter Seventeen

Nervous waiting for Max to arrive, I changed into jeans and a T-shirt, drank several cups of complimentary Twinings tea, and wolfed a whole package of HobNobs digestive biscuits, regretting the mess the crumbly cookie made on the freshly vacuumed carpet. A tap at the door sent me flying to open it.

It was Max.

"Hey." I brushed the crumbs off my GOBSMACKED! BY THE U.K. T-shirt.

"Hey."

"So George found you?"

"Yeah." Max's face registered no pleasure at seeing me. In fact, he looked a little shattered.

"She didn't grill you about why you were in London, did she?" I asked.

"She's not stupid. She's probably figured it out."

"The MI6 stuff?"

"No. The Morgan Abbott stuff."

"Oh."

He resisted slightly before allowing me to drag him into the room, where he stood a few paces away, arms folded in front like a barrier.

His silence was making me so nervous, I started babbling. "Okay, Max, here's the thing. Trevor just grabbed me."

"And started kissing you." Max's voice was flat.

"Yes! It was beyond gross, too." I shuddered at the memory. "I was trying to get him to back off, but he was being a complete tool. He has a bizarre idea that because he's the PM's son and I'm the president's daughter, that we're *supposed* to be together."

"That's not the way it looked to me." Max's stony expression hardened.

"You have to believe me." I could feel the tears threatening. I swallowed hard. "I would never do anything like that. I promise, Max. He just attacked me, lips first."

Max's expression changed from stony to furious. "Maybe I should pay Trevor a little visit and teach him some manners."

"Don't worry, I already did. Let's say he won't be able to smell too well for a while." I explained about my collision with Trevor's nose. "Honestly, the whole situation got stupid so fast."

Max didn't reply. I held my breath. "Did you really punch him?" he asked, and broke into a grin.

I let out a huge sigh of relief.

"Well, it was sort of an accident. But still completely satisfying. Trevor Eckley was being a jerk."

"Spitfire," Max murmured, and gathered me close.

Mmm-hm. Kissing Max totally wiped away the memory of Trevor's ookey kiss.

After a few minutes, we reluctantly broke apart. "I forgot to tell you," I said. "In another Morgan-related disaster, Brittany has threatened to send the photo of us to the gossip rags the minute she lands Stateside. No cell-phone reception or the deed would have already been done."

"What set her off this time?"

"Oh, who knows?" I decided not to tell him about the wrestling match I'd gotten into with Brits. Learning that his girlfriend was in two violent altercations in the same day might have been a tad too much info. "She lives to torture me, and she knows the trouble we'd be in if anyone found out about us."

Max sighed.

"Morg . . . maybe we should cool it a little."

Whaaa?

"We are breaking all kinds of rules," he went on. "And I hate having to sneak around. You should be living in the spotlight, dating a guy who fits into your lifestyle. I mean, I know I'm not exactly perfect boyfriend material for the president's daughter. I'm just a working stiff who is still paying off my student loans. I'm not sure I'm what's best for you."

"Maybe you should let me be the judge of who the president's daughter should be dating." I searched his eyes. "Are you telling me you want to date someone less complicated?"

At that, Max's sweet smile rippled over his face. "Nah. My life would be boring without a Tornado ripping it all to pieces every so often."

Aww! I draped my arms around his neck and brought him in for another passionate kiss. The kiss was different somehow. He was holding back. Then he relaxed.

After a long moment, I pulled away. "Hey, you had the interview with the Secret Intelligence Service today! How'd it go?"

"Pretty good, I think. I won't know their answer for a couple of days yet, but I passed the background checks. I think I have a shot at it."

"Excellent." I hugged him again. But deep inside, I still wasn't sure I wanted Max to get the job. We'd already been shoved far apart as it was. Max working for the British government would only widen the chasm.

Suddenly the door to the hotel room burst open, and Hannah and Prince Richard lurched inside.

"Oh my god!" Hannah cried. "The paparazzi are going nuts down in the street in front of the hotel. I've never seen anything like it, even in D.C. Rich had to have the helicopter land on the helipad on the roof of the hotel so we could avoid them."

"Londoners breed up an aggressive paparazzi," Prince Richard said. Good lord, the heir to the British throne got more smoking with every passing day, even when *royally* annoyed. His rumpled black curls and sapphire eyes were so *GQ* he'd make most male supermodels envious. "They've been following us all day."

"They were waiting for us at the helipad this morning and they never let up." Hannah blew a lock of her disheveled hair out of her eyes. "Morgan and I talked about going to the theater tonight, but I'm not sure I could face running the gauntlet again. I'm nearly blinded from camera flashes."

"Why don't we all stay in tonight?" I suggested. "Mom will be busy with official dinners, so I'm free. Max?"

"I'm free, too. Tell you the truth, I'm bushed. A night in sounds great."

"Brilliant, Morgan." The prince looked pleased. "Scotland Yard wasn't too happy about closing half the roads in the West End theater district for security purposes anyway."

"Hans?"

Hannah was already kicking off her boots.

I called George to let her know we'd be staying in tonight and not to disturb us. While Max and Prince Richard settled in to watch a soccer match on TV (Richard called it "football"—too cute!) and Hannah whisked herself into the opulent bathroom suite for a shower, I called room service. I had to be sneaky about what to order. Weird as it sounded, tabloid spies lurked in kitchens and custodial quarters hoping to pick up juicy tidbits on celebrities that they could sell to bottom-feeding tabloids and bloggers. We were hiding Prince Richard, the biggest celebrity in Great Britain, in our hotel suite. I didn't want to give away the fact that he hadn't left the premises yet. I also wasn't keen on broadcasting Max's presence to the Secret Service. And I wouldn't have put it past Brittany to nose around. So I ordered one portion of spaghetti Bolognese, hold the sauce, a side of peanut butter, grilled chicken for two, a shrimp cocktail with a side of sriracha hot sauce, and a large mesclun salad. I raided the suite's minibar for peanuts and found a couple of limes in the massive fruit basket the prime minister had sent us upon our arrival.

Once the food arrived, I got to work whipping up a quick Thai-inspired meal. Grilled chicken and shrimp got tossed in peanut butter, hot sauce, lime juice, and served over the pasta. The salad on the side, sprinkled with peanuts and orange slices from the fruit basket, completed the meal.

Hannah emerged from the bathroom completely refreshed. "Whoa, that smells good. Is that a specialty of the hotel?"

"Nope, it's a Morgan special." Proudly I served up the Thai chicken and shrimp. "I didn't want to tip off the press that we had more than two people up here, so I threw this together."

Richard took a bite. "It's delicious. And . . . hot . . ." He started coughing.

"Too much sriracha?" I asked anxiously.

"Not for me," Max said, taking a big bite. "It's perfect."

Warmth stole through me. It was silly to feel so pleased about improvising a meal for my friends, but there was nothing better than the satisfaction, the magic really, of creative cooking. It almost felt normal, just four friends chilling—in a five-star hotel with a gazillion Secret Service and MI6 personnel right outside the door. At least it was the closest I ever got to normal.

"Hold up," Hannah said. "I think we could improve the ambiance in here." She dug into her massive handbag and pulled out a rose-colored silk scarf and threw it over the lamp. The garish hotel light mellowed to a lovely glow.

"Ah, domestic bliss," Richard said. He stretched his long legs out over the coffee table and tucked into the food.

"Sure is." Max drew me down into the space next to him. I settled into the crook of Max's shoulder with a contented sigh, while Hannah snuggled next to Richard.

I wished every evening could be like this: great food, laughs, good times with friends . . . and without the pressures of celebrity to worry about.

Max tightened his arm around me.

Yep. Life was good.

Chapter Eighteen

The phone's jangle cut rudely into my sleep. I cracked open my eyes in the murky early-morning gloom. The four of us had stayed up late last night, laughing and playing a stupid card game until Richard's entourage, which had been hanging with the presidential security team, called the prince's private mobile line to remind him that he had a royal family function first thing in the morning. He and Hannah said good-bye to each other for, like, forever. Max had given me a kiss that rocked me to my toes before he, too, disappeared into the night.

The phone shrieked again.

"Answer it," Hannah moaned from her bed. She pulled a pillow over her ears so that only her eye mask showed.

I knocked the phone off the hook and groped for the handset.

"Morgan? It's Courtney Richardson."

"Uh . . . who?" Sleep fuddled my brain.

"I'm the deputy communications director on the president's rapid-response team."

I sat bolt upright in bed. This was not going to be good.

"I'll be over to your room in thirty minutes. Meanwhile, send someone down from your security detail to collect today's newspapers."

My mouth dried. "What's going on? Is Mom okay?"

"I'll explain when I get there. Don't worry, it has nothing to do with your mother."

Whew.

Then I realized if it had nothing to do with Mom, it had everything to do with me.

George arrived ten minutes later with a copy of several British newspapers. By now Hannah had crawled out of bed and we sat nervously among the clutter left over from last night's party.

"It's not good." George handed me a copy of the *Sun*.

The headline screamed across the front page: MORGAN ABBOTT'S FISTS OF FURY! along with a grainy photo of Trevor Eckley and his swollen nose. The caption breathlessly related, "London hottie Trevor Eckley was the unlucky recipient of a bloody nose from presidential wild child Morgan Abbott. Unnamed sources claimed the U.S. president's daughter, in London on an official state visit, became uncontrollably enraged for an unknown reason and landed a direct hit on the nose of the prime minister's son. . . ."

"Oh god," Hannah groaned.

"This is terrible!" I wailed. "Hitting Trevor was an accident. And look at the photo they dug up of me!" Inset into the blown-up photo of Trevor's nose (which in all honesty looked Photoshopped to make his bruise seem worse than it was) was a tiny photo of me in my tacky *Rent* costume, the one that hit the tabloids a few weeks ago and made it look like I was a sleazoid in everyday life.

"I'm not talking about that. I'm talking about this!" Hannah pointed to another headline: HAS PRINCE RICHARD SETTLED ON A LADY-LOVE AT LAST?

In contrast to my crazy-ass photo, Hannah was the picture of jetsetting glam as she was being helped out of the helicopter by Prince Richard, devastatingly handsome in his leather jacket and knit skullcap. "Is this our future queen?" the photo caption read. "Hannah Davis, best pals with President Abbott's daughter, could be considered American royalty. But really, Rich, an American?"

"Oh boy," I whispered.

A second later Mom rolled in with Humberto and a gray-haired no-nonsense woman who introduced herself as deputy communications director Courtney Richardson.

"I think Morgan should address these concerns

head-on," Courtney was saying to my mom. "Get her in front of the scandal instead of chasing it. That's the quickest way to derail the internet snowball effect and keep the bad PR from getting out of control."

"Absolutely not." Mom shook her head vehemently. "I don't want to throw Morgan to the wolves for something she didn't do."

"Actually, Mom, I did punch Trevor in the nose," I offered weakly.

"That's not at issue *at the moment*, sweetie." Mom brushed it off, but left the impression we'd be talking about the incident later. "Humberto. Thoughts?"

Humberto had been tapping his knuckle against his chin while he regarded me. I'm sure he was wishing I'd never come on this trip, but if anyone knew how to put out a fire quickly, it was Mom's chief of staff. "I think she should respond to the allegations," he said unexpectedly. "Let her tell her side of the story before others do it for her."

"The press conference would turn into a zoo, and you both know it," Mom said. "I don't want Morgan subjected to so much harassment from the media. Once you open the gate, you can't put the horse back in. The media would never leave her alone if we start giving access."

"They aren't leaving her alone now," Courtney pointed out.

"Remember, we need to control the message given to the press," Humberto added. "Not the other way around."

"Morgan is not a politician!" Mom said angrily. "She's my daughter, and I'm going to protect her from these media jackals come hell or high water—"

I stood up. "I'd like to talk to the press."

The three of them stared at me.

Mom broke the surprised silence. "Out of the question."

"I need to, Mom. Otherwise, the press will be free to make up any other stories they want about me. At least I'll have my side out there."

Mom draped her arm around me. "Oh, honey. Are you sure? Journalists are vultures who want to pick our bones clean."

"Yeah, but this is the British press. Maybe they won't be as vicious because I'm an American?"

"Don't be so sure about that," Courtney said darkly. "They might be vicious *because* you are. Foreign reporters don't always like Americans."

"I'd like to speak to the reporters, too," Hannah interjected. "I can't stand the thought that Rich is getting his love life looted because of one date."

Courtney nodded briskly. I got the sense she was someone who didn't like to waste time. "Okay, if it's a go, I'll set up a press conference for this afternoon. We'll get you both some boot-camp media training. And I'll make sure we limit the questioning, Sara. Promise."

"Well, if it's the only way to squelch the media frenzy, then I guess we have no choice. Proceed."

While Mom, Courtney, and Humberto discussed the details, George quietly approached Hannah and handed her a slip of paper. She glanced at it, then put a shaky hand to her mouth.

"What is it?" I asked. Hannah looked awful.

"It's from Buckingham Palace. I've been asked"—she swallowed hard—"to 'please abstain from contacting Prince Richard due to unforeseen scheduling issues.' Unforeseen scheduling issues? What does that mean?"

Mom and I exchanged concerned glances, while Courtney and Humberto moved politely out of earshot. "It means that the queen would prefer if you do not see her grandson again," Mom explained gently. "I'm so sorry, Hannah."

"Oh." Hannah pressed her lips together. "I get it. I'm not good enough to date Rich because I'm not a royal."

Distress lit Mom's eyes, but she'd never skirt the truth. "I'm afraid so."

I started to go to her. "Hannah—"

Hannah held up her hand to check me. "It's okay, Morgan. I just need a minute." Tears started to roll down her cheeks, and Mom and I didn't stop her as she fled to the bathroom.

The PR boot camp Courtney set up lasted from breakfast until lunch. She drummed into our heads the importance of using slow, controlled gestures or, better still, to keep our hands folded in our laps. She forbade OMG!-type slang and advised us not to be tempted to fill the silences. Answer the question and then stop talking. We practiced our "key messages," as Courtney called them. She assured us that the media couldn't quote anything we didn't say. "Choose your words carefully," Courtney said, and glanced at me.

In short, she tried to turn us into media-savvy robots in under four hours. She told us to wear conservative suits with minimal makeup. Even Hannah's love of outrageous jewelry had been tamed—she was all about the concept of damage control and was paying close attention to every-thing Courtney told her. I knew she was hoping that if she did everything just right, maybe she could see Prince Rich-ard again.

The press conference had been set up in the hotel's opulent Regency-style banquet room. Journalists, photog-raphers, and camera crews mobbed the joint all the way to the walls. In the anteroom, Courtney and one of her aides took a head count of the prominent British journalists and camera crews from the *Guardian*, *The Times*, *BBC News*, and *CNN International*.

And Brittany Whittaker's smug face popped out of the sea of strangers. No way would she pass up an opportunity to see me humiliated.

Mom arrived by a back route just before the news conference was set to start. "Nervous?" she asked.

"Nah. I've fielded press conferences before. At least this time I can do it as myself and not as the president of the United States."

Mom winked at me. Last month, disguised as Mom, I had to hold down the fort on an impromptu press conference when Mom had gotten stuck at Camp David negotiating a cease-fire in Africa. I did a pretty good job, I think. At least, no one found out about the impersonation, which counted for a lot.

Courtney interrupted us. "They're ready, Morgan."

"Showtime, sweetie." Mom smoothed my hair affectionately.

"Showtime," I repeated.

Hannah and I entered the banqueting area calmly and with our heads held high, per instructions. Cameras flashed and video recorders whirred while we sat behind the skirted table. Courtney insisted on the draping to hide any nervous twitches our legs might make. I had to hand it to Mom, she'd found another gem staffer in her deputy communications director of rapid response.

I scanned the room, getting more nervous by the minute. Maybe this wasn't such a stellar idea. Then I saw Max. He stood at the back wall partially hidden by video equipment and members of various camera crews, but he stared right at me. He flashed a thumbs-up, and I relaxed.

After a few preliminary remarks, Courtney said, "We'll open the floor for questions now. Yes, you first." She pointed.

A man with tons of ear piercings stood up. "Clive Willowby, *Daily Mail*. Morgan, how long have you been dating the prime minister's son?"

I forced my mouth into what I hoped was a winning smile. "I'm not dating the prime minister's son. We're friends, that's all."

"You Americans have a funny way of showing friendship, by the corker you landed on his nose."

Titters. Giggles.

"Trevor's injury came about purely by accident," I said serenely. "I couldn't help it if his nose slammed into my knuckles."

Hearty chuckles.

"Honestly, it was an accident. Still, it shouldn't have

happened. I apologize to Trevor Eckley, the prime minister's office, and the nation of Great Britain for the fuss I caused. Most especially, I apologize to British journalists for having to cover this pretty lame story."

Roars of laughter now.

Another journalist stood. "Morgan, if not Trevor, are you seeing anyone special?"

I sat back in my chair. Courtney hadn't prepared me for this. I swallowed. I wanted to shout from the rooftop that, yes, I was seeing Special Agent Max Jackson. But I couldn't, not without consequences. I regained my composure. "No, I'm not seeing anyone special."

It hurt to say it, but what hurt even more was the look on Max's face. He knew I couldn't answer honestly, but I could still tell my response stung. No one special. He gave me a weak smile and I tried to smile back, shifting my gaze so no one else would notice Max.

Another reporter hopped to her feet. "Jemima Jones, *Telegraph*. Question for Miss Davis. How close are you to Prince Richard?"

"We're good friends." Hannah kept her voice cool and her manner regal.

"Have you two been dating long?" someone from the back yelled.

"We met when the prince visited Washington, D.C."

Hannah didn't fill in all the blanks for the journalist, as per Courtney's instructions. We'd been prepped to give minimal answers.

"Do you think you're going to be the next queen of England?"

Hannah gave an incredulous laugh. "It's a pretty wide leap from friendship to becoming the queen of England, don't you think?"

Oh snap! Hannah had turned the question back on the reporter. She was knocking it out of the park!

A woman with aggressively plucked eyebrows and a chic aubergine suit raised her pen to be called upon. "Lulu MacGregor, *British Vogue*. Who are you wearing, Morgan?"

That's when I knew the tide had turned.

The rest of the session consisted of questions about how we were enjoying our stay in London, which West End shows we were considering attending, and random queries on our favorite British foods. I scanned the room to see how Brittany was taking this turn of events, but she was nowhere to be found.

Whatever.

Now I searched for Max, but he was gone, too.

The press conference had exhausted Hannah and me, and we crashed in the hotel room. I was dying to see Max, but we both knew we couldn't risk it—not while I was once again under the media microscope.

George ordered us room service for dinner, but neither Hannah nor I was the slightest bit hungry. We were in one of the greatest cities in the world but we couldn't enjoy it. We went to bed early, wrung out from our ordeal and missing our boyfriends.

It was hard to believe that just last night the four of us were chillin' when tonight that safe and comfortable feeling felt so far away.

The next morning, I asked for all the newspapers to be brought in.

"Hannah, wake up," I called.

"What?" she answered grouchily from under a pile of rumpled bed linens. Hannah had stayed up half the night emailing Richard from the hotel's business center—but so far no dice. He wasn't answering her messages, nor the calls she made from the hotel room's phone to his private mobile line.

"You'll want to see this." I held up the front page of the *Daily Mail*'s Entertainment section: AMERICAN GIRLS: MORGAN ABBOTT AND HANNAH DAVIS JUST WANNA HAVE FUN.

The photo spread featured a couple of semidecent official White House shots of me, supplied by Courtney, no doubt, plus a nice one of Hannah and me together at the press conference. The story itself was what Mom would call a cream-puff piece, with plenty of favorable angles.

"And listen to this. It says, 'Miss Davis is the epitome of American chic, a young Halle Berry in the making. Her composed responses to our questions were certainly light-years ahead of her peers.' A young Halle Berry! Aren't you dying over that?"

"I guess." Hannah hauled herself up and reached for the nearest paper. She eyed an image of her with sun-glasses and a fuchsia trench coat that made her pop out of the crowd while she strode through a busy London thor-oughfare. "I wish Rich would call . . . or email . . . or *anything.*"

"He will, don't worry."

"I'm not sure about that. We're talking the royal fam-ily here. Rich says it's hard to go against family tradition. I need to make it clear to him that I don't have any thoughts whatsoever of becoming a future queen. I mean, my main goal right now is to get accepted to Parsons School for Design—not to become royalty! Why can't people leave us alone? It feels like the whole world is trying to split us up. And . . . I miss him."

She dropped her head into her hands.

I felt awful. Hannah and Prince Richard were only

trying to live a normal life. Why did the press have to ruin everything within the pressure cooker of celebrity?

"I tell you what. Why don't we hang together today? We can do whatever you want. Shopping, sightseeing, you name it."

"Don't you have plans with Max?"

"He'll understand." At least, I hoped so. Hannah was my best friend. She needed me now.

I prodded Hannah out of bed and sent her down to the hotel's day spa for a massage and facial, my treat. Then I called Mom's deputy secretary in charge of her itinerary to arrange a surprise for Hannah that I knew would get her mind off Richard. I hated using the power of the presidency for special treatment, but this was my BFF we were talking about.

I risked a call to Max from the hotel room's phone. It went straight to voice mail. I had to leave a cryptic message in case someone was listening: "Change in plans. Out with Hannah all day. Sorry." I hoped he could read between the lines. Hannah needed me.

The plans came together fairly quickly. The only thing I had to worry about was the continued unwelcome presence of Brittany Whittaker. If she so much as sniffed a clue that Hannah and I were going somewhere cool, she'd use her blackmail to tag along and destroy our fun. Why did

Chapter Nineteen

Leave it to Brittany to give ruining my day her bestest effort *evah*, as the British would say. If she put that much energy into being *nice*, she might have a decent chance at being a human being.

Hannah and I headed out later that morning with George and a few Secret Service colleagues in tow. As expected, Brittany "just happened" to be loitering down in the lobby by the concierge desk. When she saw us, she immediately bailed midsentence on the über-tolerant concierge and tagged after us. "Where are you two going?"

"Just some sightseeing," I said offhandedly. "Could you excuse us? We're in a hurry."

She fell in step beside us anyway. "Must be big if you're taking the full security team."

I shrugged. "Nah. You know how it is, daughter of the president, foreign country and all. Nothing out of the ordinary."

"Doesn't seem that way to me."

"Well, it isn't always about you, is it, Brits?" Hannah put in.

"Ooo, cranky. You still upset about your royal boyfriend dumping you, Davis? Frankly, who could blame the guy? Maybe I should get in touch with him and show him what a classy American girl is all about."

Hannah turned around to let Brittany have it.

"Stick to the plan," I whispered to her.

Hannah ground her teeth together and nodded grimly. We continued a few more paces until we came to the revolving doors in the hotel lobby.

"I'll see you later, okay, Morg?" Hannah called.

"Sure, we'll catch up then. Have a good time."

Hannah peeled away down a corridor leading to a different street-level exit, while the Secret Service detail stayed with me. Brittany checked her step, not sure who to follow.

I swept out to the parking garage, wrinkling my nose at the smell of diesel and motor oil. A fleet of unmarked limos had taken over the deck. "Is she still following?" I whispered to George.

George glanced behind. "Affirmative. Just like you suspected. Here we go."

George gave a prearranged signal to her fellow agents and I hopped inside one of the unmarked limos.

"Hi, Mom!"

My mother looked up from reading a brief. "Hi, honey. Did you get everything arranged for your day with Hannah?"

"Yup. I've got everything under control," I said. "See you later."

"Have fun."

I crawled through the backseat of the limo and slipped out the opposite door. Then I scooted between two unmarked cars until I came to the one I wanted. Gently I cracked open the door. George was inside waiting for me. As soon as I inched in and settled on the seat, George muttered into her com: "Tornado's on the move."

Limos began backing up and moving out in a flurry of squealing tires. Through the smoked glass, I could see Brittany standing stock-still in confusion in the middle of the garage, unsure of which limo I'd gotten into.

The limo eased out into traffic and around the block to the service entrance at the rear of the hotel. Hannah emerged from the doorway and hopped inside. "Did we lose her?" she asked.

"Worked like a charm." I allowed myself to feel a little smug. I'd outmaneuvered the CEO of underhanded manipulations and I felt that I deserved to bask in the glow of that little victory for the rest of the day.

The limo fought the traffic through Charing Cross as we headed to Covent Garden and the heart of London's West End theater district. Tourists flooded the sidewalks. Row after row of shabbily majestic theaters, cool boutiques, and the occasional pub lined the streets. Buskers played guitar for money, artsy Londoners mixed in with picture-snapping tourists, and the whole area reeked of fun.

Hannah grew visibly more excited. "Wow, I'd love to go backstage at one of these musicals," she said, practically bouncing in her seat.

"Oh yeah?"

"You know it. The costumes, the staging. The fabulous makeup! I'd die."

"Don't die. I'd like to keep my BFF around for a little longer."

"What?"

"Check it out."

From Shaftesbury Avenue, the limo turned into an alley behind the Lyric Theatre, where a group of theater people had gathered.

Hannah started freaking out. "Oh my god! Is that Sally Gordon, the star of *Scheherazade*? And Chaco Bruce, who originated the role of the Sultan? I luuurve him!"

"I thought you could use some cheering up, so I arranged a special backstage tour before the matinee showing."

"Morgan! Oh my god! Just . . . omigod!" Hannah flung her arms around my neck and nearly strangled me.

The rest of the afternoon was a blast. The cast and crew treated us to an insiders' tour backstage and they even offered to let us help with the matinee performance. The makeup artists took Hannah under their wing and she got to help transform Sally Gordon from a fair-skinned blonde into the sultry Arabian beauty Scheherazade.

"You're a natural at this," I heard Sally tell Hannah while she helped ease the long black wig over her head, making sure Sally's blond hair didn't tangle under the wig cap and sliding bobby pins gently around her hairline. "Usually I want to weep or scream after donning this wretched wig. But you have the right touch."

The happy glow on Hannah's face meant she'd temporarily forgotten about her troubles with Prince Richard.

I exchanged looks with George, who nodded back in acknowledgment. She'd had the theater swept for security clearance in record time so we could give Hannah this experience. I owed her and the office of the presidency big-time.

Chaco Bruce, the actor who played the romantic male lead (oh lord, the dude was a stone-cold fox!), approached. I tried not to spontaneously combust. "I heard you've been in a few plays yourself," he remarked.

"Just high school productions," I answered. Did I sound like a gibbering idiot because Chaco's deep blue eyes reminded me of Max's? "Nothing as epic as a professionally staged musical, though."

"Would you like to find out what it's like?"

"What do you mean?"

"We could fit another extra into the big ensemble pieces. You wouldn't have to sing, just stand in the back and pretend you're part of the Sultan's entourage."

"Are you serious? I'd love to!"

Curtain call was in twenty minutes, so I was hurried into a purple silk kaftan, pointy slippers, and a turban loaded with costume jewels. Hannah dusted a deep bronzer over my skin and glued a fake mustache over my lip.

Nerves ate me up as the curtain rose, but one of the other chorus Arabians kept an eye on me and made sure I hit my mark so I didn't interfere with the principal cast members. The lights blinded me at first, but I quickly got used to them—as well as the unique smell of actors baking inside the elaborate costumes. Adrenaline pumped through me when the applause of a full house swelled along with the music from the orchestra playing in the pit in front of the stage.

The finale included all the cast members mourning the death of Scheherazade. My chorus partner had placed me at the very end of the stage so I could be the first one off after curtain call. One by one the principal actors took their bows to a standing ovation. Then the chorus lined up to bow. I bent at the waist and my turban toppled off my head onto the stage.

I should have warned the stage manager that I was prone to disaster.

"It's the president's daughter!" someone in the audience yelled.

"Huzzah, Morgan Abbott! Bravo! Bravo!"

One of the chorus boys took my hand and led me to the front of the stage. He gave me a kiss on the cheek and raised my hand to the audience.

The noise in the theater was deafening, but the cheers were friendly. I pasted a smile on my face and, turban in hand, took another bow to renewed cheers. Thank gawd the British had a sense of humor. Later, I'd probably be able to watch myself on YouTube, if the massive amount of cell-phone cameras lighting up the audience were any indication.

Afterward, I met up with Hannah as she finished swapping makeup tips with the head makeup artist. "Wasn't this a total blast?" she said. "I'm so going to do this after college. By the way, you looked good out there! The spotlight suits you."

"I've had a ton of practice with the spotlight," I said.

When *wasn't* I in the spotlight? Truth be told, I was getting tired of it. I was ready to be plain ol' Morgan Abbott and give the spotlight a rest.

Sally Gordon recommended a trendy Asian/tapas fusion restaurant around the corner toward Piccadilly Circus. Ten minutes before we arrived, George called management to reserve a table in the quietest corner. As promised, Kit-Kue Klub's decor mashed a weird mix of animal prints and Japanese anime, but somehow the whole thing worked. I loved the edgy kitschiness right away. Luckily, the patrons and management at KitKue Klub were used to celebrities popping in, and our arrival with the security detail was met with a collective yawn.

"Wow, check out the menu," I said to Hannah, who sighed in ecstasy over the fabulous fringed leopard print club chairs. "The ahi pizza sounds killer. I'd never think of pairing sushi and pizza."

Hannah wrinkled her nose. "Sounds gross to me. I'll stick with the Asian fries and duck salad, thanks."

I ordered the pizza, kimchee fried rice, salmon carpaccio, and a molten lava chocolate cake to appease Hannah.

She raised her passionfruit mocktail served in a twisty martini glass. "Thanks for the day, Morgan. You really pulled out all the stops, and I know what a hassle it must have been to arrange a day at the theater."

"Well, to be fair, I came up with the idea, but George and Mom's aides did most of the work. You'd do the same for me if I needed cheering up. Besides, you've stuck with me through some major issues. Brittany, impersonating my mom, guy troubles—"

"When you put it that way, yeah, you owe me big-time."

We giggled and clinked our glasses together.

"Seriously," Hannah said. "Thanks. Spending time backstage today made me realize that I *belong* in the visual arts. I'd love to be able to dress people up for a living."

I toyed with a piece of sushi. "I wish I was as certain about my future as you are about yours."

Surprise flicked across her face. "You mean you don't want to go to college? I thought that's why you were stressing out about your SAT so much . . . so you could get into a good school."

"C'mon, Hans. I'm not really Ivy League material, am I?" I gave a hollow chuckle.

"All right, Morgan. Dish."

I could never hide much from Hannah.

"Well, what I'd really like to do is become a chef." Admitting it felt like taking off in Air Force One—the rush and then flying.

"Chef? Like, cook food and stuff?"

"Yeah. Cook food. But really cool food like this,

surprising food that makes people happy. And I want to own my own restaurant someday. Something fun and trendy, constantly evolving. I'd love that."

"Then why don't you go for it?"

"Hello, daughter of the president here. I'm supposed to sit on the board of my father's corporation or go into politics. Or at the very least become a civil rights lawyer or aid worker with the U.N."

"Listen, Morgan. It sounds corny, but you should follow your heart. Otherwise, you'll be miserable."

I sighed. I wished I could be sure my heart knew what it was talking about. I felt pulled in so many different directions, I didn't know which way to go.

A waitress in a neo-punk outfit set the molten lava chocolate cake in front of us. Hannah picked up her fork with enthusiasm. "What do you wanna bet Brittany is camped out in the lobby of the hotel waiting for us?"

"Probably whining to the concierge that we ditched her."

"Which we did."

We slapped a high five over the cake.

Chapter Twenty

The next morning, Hannah discreetly left the hotel room early to have breakfast in the tearoom in the lobby so I could beautify before Max arrived. We'd arranged a secret visit through a series of cryptic phone messages.

I'd never make it as a spy. But I knew Max was spy material. As much as I wanted Max to land this MI6 job, I selfishly *didn't* want it to happen even more. How awful.

I'd just swiped some bronzer on my cheeks and got my hair fluffed when the tap came at the door. I opened it and hauled Max in for a big hug.

"Easy, Morg. You're strangling me," he laughed.

"I missed you lots." God, he smelled great and looked even better, despite his blah suit.

"Missed you, too. Are we . . . alone?"

I grinned. "Yeah."

"So where's Hannah?" he asked.

"Down in the lobby tearoom learning to love Marmite and toast."

Max shuddered. "Why would anyone ruin a good piece of toast with that horrible salty goo?"

"Hey, I like it! Expand your food horizons."

"Bangers and mash is about as far as I want my food horizons to expand. Is Hannah feeling better about the Richard thing?"

"No. She's putting on a brave face, but I can tell she's still upset that he won't talk to her."

"The palace probably issued a noncommunication edict." Max and I plopped down on the sofa, snuggling together. "Richard must be waiting for things to cool down before contacting Hannah again."

"Well, it's tearing her up."

"I'm sure it is." Max's face settled into a serious expression. "It can be hard dating a celebrity. The security, the subterfuge—"

"I'm tired of all the sneaking around, too." I sighed and unglued myself from him a bit. "Why don't I tell my mom about us? She could talk to the head of the Secret Service about that stupid fraternization regulation between agents and protectees. I'm sure she could work something out."

"Out of the question," Max said sharply. "I would never put the president in the position of using her power to ask for a special favor, and neither should you."

"Hey, don't get angry. I'm only trying to think of a way we can see each other more often. I hate the sneaking as much as you do." More, in fact. Hiding my relationship with Max from my parents was really wearing me down.

"I'm not angry." Max sighed and ran a hand through his short-cropped hair. "I'm frustrated. I've never been good at lying. And it feels like every time we're together, we have to lie to make it happen."

"Whoa. That's a pretty negative way of putting it."

"It's the truth, isn't it?"

"But it's worth it. At least to me, it is. Don't you feel the same way?"

But Max said nothing.

"Max?"

"I don't know anymore," he said.

I felt like someone had punched me in the stomach.

Max looked wrecked, but he took a deep breath and continued. "You should be able to enjoy your senior year without worrying about sneaking around. I know it's eating you up hiding me from your mother. You should find someone you can bring home to meet your parents and not have to sneak around with in boiler rooms."

"I don't want to find anyone else. Why are you saying these things?"

"Because we should face the facts, Morgan. This isn't any way to have a relationship. We can't go on like this."

I tried to speak, but no sound came out. Having this conversation was turning me inside out. It hurt more than I could have imagined. What happened to our happy morning? Finally I forced some words. "Are you breaking up with me?"

Max opened his mouth, but before he could speak, a tap came at the door.

"It's gotta be Hannah," I said. My voice sounded weird, like razor-wire. Maybe because a huge lump had ballooned in my throat.

"Hang on." Max opened the door that connected the bedroom to the lounge suite and slid inside. "We shouldn't take any chances."

It was then I had a moment of clarity. As horrible as it was, Max was right. Totally, utterly right.

We couldn't keep going on this way.

I swiped my eyes with the back of my hand to clear away the tears before I opened the door. George stood in the hall, hands folded before her in the Secret Service stance.

"Hey, George. What's up?" I hoped I looked nonchalant.

George's face betrayed no emotion, but her eyes flicked behind me. "The Queen's Concert at the Royal Albert Hall in a few hours. That's what's up. You need to start getting ready."

The lump in my throat threatened to strangle me. "I'm, uh, not in the mood to go to the concert. Can I beg out?"

"You want me to tell the president of the United States that you don't want to go to a concert hosted by the queen of England? A concert that is being held in your mother's honor? Really, Morgan?"

Good point.

"You and Hannah need to be ready to go by noon. I'll be back then with the security detail to escort you both."

"Fine," I muttered. "I'll be ready."

I shut the door on George and hurried to the lounge. "Max?"

No answer. There was another door in there that led out into the corridor. He must have slipped away.

A sense of desperation swept over me. I *had* to work it out with Max. I couldn't lose him now. I had to make him understand that we belonged together.

I couldn't nurse my hurt over the growing rift between Max and me for long, though, because Hannah burst through the door fired up with excitement. "Morg, I've got it!"

"Got what? By the way, George was here. We have to get ready for the concert this afternoon. We only have a couple hours."

"Concert, schmoncert, *listen*! I've figured out a way to

get Rich to talk to me!"

"Really? You going to storm Buckingham Palace or something?"

"Better." A great big smile broke over her face. "You are going to impersonate the president and talk the queen into letting me see him."

I paused, waiting for her to say "Psyche!"

But she didn't.

"This is a joke, right? Too much Marmite on your toast has turned your brain to mush."

"I'm serious, Morgan. I've thought through everything. I've still got the wig in my makeup trunk. All we need is a copy of the dress your mom bought at Harrods the other day, and we'll be all set."

"Hold up! Who said I was agreeing to your plan? Impersonate my mom so I can plead your cause to the queen? It's insane!"

"Morgan." Hannah's face dissolved into agony. "I need to see Richard. I know you can charm the queen into relaxing the restrictions, even if only to allow us to talk for a few minutes. I need closure with him if nothing else."

I bit my lip. Being on the edge of losing Max for good made me understand exactly how Hannah felt. Plus, Hannah had always been there for me and *never, ever* asked for favors as BFF of the president's daughter.

I couldn't let her down.

"All right," I said. "I'll do it. But we're treading on thin ice here. If I get caught impersonating Mom while talking to the queen, it'll mean scandal up the wazoo. We are risking my mom's presidency."

"It's just for a few minutes with an audience of one," Hannah promised. "I've got it all figured out."

"I hope so. Or I'll be grounded in Siberia for the rest of my life."

Chapter Twenty-one

"Holy cow. The Secret Service isn't messing around," I said to George as the limo pulled around to the private entrance at the Royal Albert Hall. The security scattered throughout the round concert hall was the most insane I'd ever seen, and that was saying something. Snipers perched on the white-domed roof, concrete barriers . . . and probably every bobby in London's police force shoulder to shoulder on the sidewalk. Plus the City of London's SWAT team blocked off the surrounding streets.

"Of course we don't mess around when two heads of state and a monarch are involved," George replied. She pressed the com button on the lapel of her suit and muttered, "Tornado's whirling in."

I exchanged worried looks with Hannah, who clutched a massive leather handbag holding the wig and the look-alike gown we'd quickly purchased from Harrods. I'd need to change into both in order to impersonate Mom. Hopefully we wouldn't be searched on our way into the building, or our plan would be toast.

Pure luck gave us our first break. George scooted us around the security X-ray station set up at the entrances and whisked us down a back corridor to the box seats in the balcony.

"I need you two in place ASAP," she said. "There's too much going on to risk any security compromises."

She opened the door to our box seats. Two people were already settled in the red velvet chairs.

Ugh. Trevor Eckley. And double ugh. Brittany Whittaker. How'd that happen?

"Blimey, Morgan." Trevor rose and gave me the once-over, eyes lingering on the modest neckline of my little black dress. A faint blue bruise shadowed his nose. "You look blinding. And who is this lovely lady? Chocolate and vanilla are my favorite flavors."

Hannah recoiled like she'd seen a snake. Well, she had, of sorts. A simple gold pendant at her throat set off the dusky rose of her designer gown, so of course she looked amazing. But "chocolate and vanilla"? Gross. "This the guy you punched out, Morgan?"

"Yeah."

"He'd better behave or I'll show him how we roll Davis style."

Trevor sank back down in his chair. "You American girls certainly are touchy about compliments."

"Don't pay any attention to them, Trevor." Brittany leaned into his arm and let her silky blond hair brush his cheek. She wore a ruched periwinkle number, the neckline caked with rhinestones. "I like compliments."

Hannah's hand squeezing my arm distracted me from barfing. "There's Rich," she whispered.

Below us, a scattering of applause announced that Prince Richard had entered the royal box, which was identified by an enlarged replica of a crown hanging off the edge of the balcony. Richard wore a black tux that complimented his dark good looks and made every girl in the room swoon.

"Damn," Hannah murmured, eyes locked on him.

George leaned in from the shadows where she was discreetly stationed. "You two better sit down," she told me, hand cupped over her earpiece. "I've just heard that Foxfire is on her way."

Foxfire. Mom's Secret Service code name. She was to meet the queen for the first time minutes before they walked on stage together and welcomed the guests to the concert.

Trevor had risen and moved to the back of the box so he could take a phone call on his mobile, leaving two seats next to Brittany vacant. "Yep, sure thing." I hastily plopped down next to Brittany. Hannah eased herself into her chair, never taking her eyes off Richard.

"Basic black, huh, Morgan?" Brittany looked me up and down. "Kinda boring for the daughter of the president, isn't it?"

"What?" I'd hardly paid any attention to Brittany. Nerves were eating me up as I mentally reviewed the plan to impersonate my mother.

"Your dress. It's boring." She uttered each word slowly.

I'd promised Mom earlier that I'd pull back on the drama for the remainder of our trip, so I bit my tongue over the retort that Brittany's dress looked like a reject from Paris Hilton's closet.

"But I do like those earrings," she continued. "Very sparkly."

I fingered one of the crystal droplets dangling from my ear. Hannah had made them from Swarovski beads and silver wire. I loved them.

"They'd go really well with my dress, actually."

"Mmm," I replied. Hannah had begun to quiver in her chair as she continued to stare at Richard, and I wondered if she was holding back tears. Trevor, surprise surprise, had settled into the last vacant chair next to Hannah and picked at a hangnail, oblivious to the tension seething around him.

"I'd like to have them."

"Have what?"

"Those earrings."

I tore my gaze away from Hannah to Brittany. "You're joking, right?"

"You should know by now that I don't joke."

She wasn't kidding. She was drop-dead serious.

"Forget it. I'm not giving you my earrings. No way. No how." I was so sick of being held hostage by Brittany and her blackmail, and I had a sneaking suspicion that her extortion had given Max cold feet about me—not that I'd let Brittany find out how successful her stupid plan was in ruining my relationship with Max.

Brittany pouted. "It's a shame you aren't in a more generous mood, Abbott. I might reconsider sending the photos I have of you and your secret boyfriend if you'd only be a little nicer."

I ground my teeth together.

"Plus I might not tell the papers how horrible you've been to me this whole visit, acting like a stuck-up bitch and ditching me when I'm all alone in a foreign country. I don't know, though . . . I'm sure they'd love to hear how you've been using your status to get special favors in London."

"I haven't been doing that!"

"Oh really? Come on."

I thought about the theater district surprise I'd arranged to cheer up Hannah. When Brittany got done blabbing to the press, there was no telling what they'd think.

"Fine." I dragged the earrings off and handed them to her. "Happy?"

She unhooked her rhinestone dangles off her ears and slid mine on. "Getting there."

Hannah finally seemed to come out of her Prince Richard–induced coma. We nodded to each other. Time to put Operation Meet the Queen into play.

Hannah leaned toward Brittany and said in a confidential tone, "Hey, Brits. I think someone's crushing on you."

"What are you talking about, Davis?"

Hannah tilted her head meaningfully at Trevor sitting next to her. Trevor, mercifully, was checking his mobile for text messages, completely oblivious, though it might have helped if he looked a *little* more lovestruck. But we were improvising this part.

He's texting his friend, Hannah mouthed to her. *About you.*

"Really?"

"Yeah." Hannah glanced at Trevor stealthily to make sure he was still oblivious (he was) before she continued. "He's been asking me if you have a boyfriend."

Brittany started preening. "I have lots of boyfriends."

"Here's your chance to hook up with the prime minister's son," I put in.

Her eyes sharpened with calculation.

"You wanna switch seats with me, Brits?" Hannah half rose.

For a split second, Brittany hesitated. Then Trevor snapped his mobile shut and let his lizard eyes drift impersonally over her before they glazed in his usual self-absorbed torpor.

That settled it. She nodded.

No sooner had she taken her seat than she hit the flirt button, giggling and tossing her hair at him. "I really like that, er, shirt you're wearing," she cooed. "So sophisticated."

"Really?" Trevor pepped up a bit.

"Blue's your color."

Now Trevor fully woke from his stupor. "Got this little number at my favorite Savile Row haberdasher. Not everyone has an eye for quality, though. You've got bang-on taste. For an American." He threw me a dark look.

Brittany giggled.

Ugh.

Once they became absorbed in out-flirting each other, Hannah and I snuck to the back of the box where George sat, arms folded. Watching us. "We, uh, need to use the bathroom," I told her.

"Both of you? At the same time?"

"We want to leave the lovebirds alone for a while." I thumbed over to Brittany and Trevor, who seemed to be getting cozier by the minute.

"Fine." George rose.

"Don't worry about coming with us," I said quickly. "The bathroom is across the corridor and we'll probably hang out there for a while until the concert starts. You know, to keep from gagging." By now Brittany was practically climbing into Trevor's lap.

George's eyes narrowed, but she sat back down. "All right. Don't take forever."

I hoped it wouldn't.

Hannah grabbed her handbag loaded with Mom's look-alike gown and the wig. We slipped out and gently let the door to the box swing shut behind us. Well-dressed guests were making their way to their box seats, but no one paid us any attention.

"Which way to backstage, do you think?" I asked Hannah.

"No clue. Let's start walking, we should find it soon enough."

We started making our way down the big circular corridor. Since we were one flight up on the Grand Tier, we dropped down a couple flights of stairs, figuring that access to backstage would be on the ground floor, level with the stage. Our feet didn't make a sound on the plush magenta carpet.

"Bingo," I said to Hannah. Next to an exit light, we found an artists-only door. We eased it open to reveal a dingy corridor loaded with banged-up trunks, dinged orchestra cases, and exposed air ducts.

"This was way easier than I thought it would be," I began.

Then I heard a soft cough behind me. I turned.

"So you were just going to the bathroom?" George shook her head. "It's not good to lie to your Secret Service agent, Morgan. Makes me not trust you."

"Uhhh . . . "

"In fact, it makes me wonder what you're up to and what your friend has in that handbag."

Busted!

George looked so scary right now. No way would I be able to talk my way out of this one.

Chapter Twenty-two

"We, er, got lost?" I offered.

"Don't insult my intelligence," George said. "Make this easy on both of us and come clean, Morgan."

Tell my Secret Service agent that I'd planned on impersonating the president of the United States so I could plead with the queen of England to let my best friend date her grandson? Riiight. "Honestly, we got lost."

"I can help you," she said unexpectedly.

Hannah and I stared at each other. Help us?

"It'll be much better if we were on the same side instead of you sneaking around and me having to cover your tracks for you. It's getting exhausting."

"You've been covering my tracks?" I echoed, stunned.

"How do you think you and Max have been able to see each other so much? I put him on the Secret Service access list at the hotel. Max is a good agent, he might be able to breach the bubble once in a while, but he's not *that* good."

My Secret Service agent had been helping me see Max all this time? Could. Not. Process.

"Let's tell her, Morgan," Hannah said. "We're wasting time."

I bit my lip, calculating. How much more trouble could I get in? Besides, Hannah was right. We *were* wasting time.

So I gave George the bare-bones outline of what Hannah and I hoped to accomplish, and as I was telling her, it sounded more nuts than ever. "Still want to help us with our crazy plan?"

George displayed remarkable self-control given what she'd just heard. "I didn't think it'd be *that* crazy."

Impressive.

"We need to get to the queen," I said. "ASAP."

"This way." George led us down a stairwell. We passed by a desk with a security checkpoint. I tensed, but George flashed her ID and we were waved through. We wandered around the musty hallways until we emerged into an area just to the left of the main stage.

"Now what?" George asked.

"We need a place where Morgan can change," Hannah said.

"Wait here."

George disappeared. "Do you think she's ratting us

out?" Hannah asked.

"I don't think so. If she wanted to, she would have put the kibosh on the whole thing earlier." But really I had no idea. Maybe George was right this minute spilling the beans to my mother. I started breaking out at the thought of the consequences, so I just stopped thinking about it. Seemed easier to go with the flow at this point.

George returned more quickly than I thought she would. "There's a vacant dressing room off stage left. At least, I think it's vacant. There's no makeup or costumes in it, just a bunch of sound cables."

Hannah gave a cheer. "Great! It should only take a couple minutes to get Morgan ready."

George stood guard outside the dressing room door while I hurried into the semiwrinkled gown. Hannah eased the bob wig over my head. "No time for wig glue or bobby pins," she muttered. "Just don't move your head around."

"Uh . . . okay. Do you have the earrings?"

Hannah handed me a pair of cubic zirconia studs that looked exactly like Mom's trademark one-carat diamond studs.

Hannah swiped some low-key lip color over my lips and a little mascara over my lashes, and stood back to survey her handiwork. "Ferosh," she pronounced. "In a presidential way, of course."

Of course. If you could call wearing a staid blue gown with a modest amount of beads along the collar and a bob-style wig ferocious.

George poked her head in. "The coms are buzzing. The queen is already here, and Foxfire is arriv . . . ing."

Hannah and I experienced the immense satisfaction of rendering my hard-core Secret Service agent speechless. She recovered quickly, though.

"The protocol for a meet and greet with the queen is pretty simple. Call her Your Majesty when you first address her, then afterward ma'am. Gently shake her extended hand if she offers it. Above all, do *not* touch her. Unless you want to be tackled by MI6 agents."

"Got it." Don't touch the queen. Should be simple enough.

"How long do you need?" George asked.

Nerves began fluttering in my stomach. "Five minutes, tops."

"I think we can only delay the president for about two, so you'd better get to the point quickly."

No problem, if I could keep from babbling insanely.

"You can do it, Morgan." Hannah gave me a thumbs-up. "I have faith in you. And I'll think of some way to stretch your two minutes into three by talking to your mom."

"Thanks, Hans."

George's com chirped. "The motorcade is pulling up to the VIP entrance," she said. "The queen is waiting for the president in the greenroom backstage with her entourage."

I took a deep breath. "Showtime."

I slipped into the greenroom through a side door, expecting to find courtiers and all sorts of security. To my surprise, the room was empty except for a dumpy woman in a satin gown a nightmarish shade of green, an MI6 agent dressed in a tuxedo, and . . . the queen.

A flash of electricity jolted through me. Now I'm pretty used to meeting celebrities, I mean, some people consider *me* a celebrity of sorts, but when the queen of England is standing in front of you, it doesn't get more surreal than that. Her grandmotherly figure filled out a silvery beaded number, and her hair was a beautiful shade of white. A modest diamond tiara was nestled on top of her snowy curls.

The queen had been fiddling with the drawstring on her silver-beaded clutch, but she looked up when I entered. "Madam President?"

The MI6 agent goggled at me, while the frumpy woman looked shocked, then annoyed. I later learned that she was the queen's main lady-in-waiting in charge of manners and royal protocol, and I'd wrecked her whole agenda.

Okay. Try not to freak out, Morgan.

"Your Majesty," I said. I remembered what George had told me about extending my hand for a gentle shake.

"We had word that the motorcade was still at the gate," the queen said. Her voice, plummy and cultured, held a note of surprise.

The MI6 agent reached for his com button.

Quickly I said, "I thought I'd slip in quietly for a moment, gather my thoughts, and break the ice before we meet formally in front of all those people."

To my relief, the queen nodded in agreement. "That's a sensible notion. I never liked all the fuss, either. Protocol seems to have been invented by men to make things more important than they are. Women leaders should stick together, and things would go much more swimmingly."

"I agree," I said. "Women should give every advantage they can to other women."

The queen gave me an odd look.

I was trying to be subtle, but the com chirping on the MI6 agent's lapel meant I didn't have that luxury. "I'll get right to the point. Usually I don't interfere in the romantic lives of my daughter and her friends, but Hannah Davis is a lovely girl. Wouldn't it be wonderful to give young love a chance to blossom without all the stodgy protocol getting in the way? It is the modern age, after all."

An unreadable emotion flickered behind the queen's

sapphire eyes, the ones her grandson had inherited. My heart sank. I thought she was totally ticked off at my presumption. I'd blown it!

"You're right, Madam President. I think the conventions of a past age can hamper the younger generation too much."

Wha?

"That's . . . great." I could barely get the words out. The MI6 agent muttered into his com, while the frumpy lady moved closer to me.

Worried that she'd start asking questions, I edged toward the door. "Would you excuse me for a moment? I need to visit the ladies' room."

The queen graciously inclined her head, and I booked out of there. With presidential dignity, of course.

I'd just about made it back to the vacant dressing room when I heard the horrible sound of coms buzzing and the general commotion caused by the imminent arrival of a head of state.

Mom swept around the corner, surrounded by Secret Service agents and staff. I sped through the dressing room door as fast as I could scoot in those patent leather pumps, but not fast enough. My eyes locked with Mom's.

And boy, *livid* did not begin to describe what I saw in them.

Chapter Twenty-three

I shut the door to the dressing room behind me and leaned against it, heart bludgeoning my rib cage. I was going to get a *colossal* reaming out over this.

I eased off the wig and told myself to chill. If I got in trouble for helping a friend, so be it. I'd take the punishment.

Hannah and George entered a few minutes later. "We totally stalled your mom," Hannah crowed, beaming with triumph. "You can thank George, she's the one who sent the Secret Service team around the back way."

George, however, wasn't smiling. "It should have bought you a few more minutes, Tornado. Did you accomplish the mission?"

"If by mission, you mean talk to the queen about letting Hannah see her grandson, I did. Fingers crossed that it works. I couldn't tell if she was convinced by my argument or being British polite."

Hannah glowed with happiness and her eyes sparkled with real hope. Her ecstatic mood would make my upcoming punishment worth the pain. I didn't have the heart to tell them that their ploy to delay my mom had failed.

"Anyway, help me out of this dress. Brittany and Trevor have to be wondering where we are by now."

"Yeah, we've been taking the longest bathroom break in history." Hannah turned me around to unzip the gown.

With Hannah's help, I became Morgan in less than five minutes. George rushed us back through the corridors to our box. "The concert is about to start," she said, listening intently to the com in her ear. "You need to be seated when that happens so the president can give you a recognition moment."

"Got it." Mom was supposed to point me out from the stage, where I was to rise and wave briefly to the crowd.

We burst into the box. "Holy hell!" Hannah squawked.

Trevor and Brittany were totally twisted together in a major lip lock. They sprang apart, panting and sweaty. Brittany's bubblegum-pink lipstick was smeared all over Trevor's face.

"Don't you know everyone can see you from up here?" I asked. "What's the matter with you two?"

I pointed to the audience below. Half the spectators were craning their necks up toward the make-out session going on in our box, while the guests in the boxes on either side of ours were either laughing or scrunching their faces in disgust over the major PDA.

"Yep, that's going to get me in trouble with the old man," Trevor drawled. He didn't look worried at all, though. Instead he wore that preening expression guys get when they've hooked up with a hottie.

Brittany hastily adjusted her rumpled dress. "People should mind their own business," she said snottily. "Besides, where have you two been? Peeing can't take that long."

"Maybe we were trying to give you and Trevor privacy." Hannah settled next to Trevor. "Don't get any ideas about me, bud."

"Wouldn't dream of it." But Trevor still couldn't resist one last ogle at Hannah's cleavage.

George leaned close to my ear. "You need to take your seat, Morgan. The concert's getting ready to start."

"Right." I sat next to Brittany, all keyed up on adrenaline. I'd pulled off a major presidential switch, and I'd spoken to the queen!

Brittany sniffed in annoyance when my leg brushed hers. "God, give me some space, you cow. And your hair looks like crap. What did you do to it in the bathroom, stick your head under the air dryer?"

I touched my hair. I'd forgotten to have Hannah brush it out when I took off the wig because we were in such a hurry.

I went on the offensive, hoping to throw her off the trail. "I'd be super nice to me if I were you. You may enjoy getting your photo in the tabloids because of your make-out session with the prime minister's son, but I doubt his dad will be all that thrilled. *Or* yours. I can either have Mom's rapid-response team work with you . . . or leave you hanging."

"Bitch," she muttered. Then she focused on my ear. "Hold on. Where'd you get those earrings?"

"What are you talking about?" I touched my ears and felt the fake diamond studs in the lobes.

"Those look exactly like the ones your mother wears. Except you weren't wearing them before. You gave *me* your earrings."

Wow. And I had actually let myself feel good about the swap for about three seconds.

The wheels in Brittany's head began to turn. "You and Hannah leave for, like, ever . . . then you come back wearing your mother's earrings. . . ."

"You'd better check yourself right now, Brits," Hannah interjected. "Remember the last time you got crazy ideas about Morgan and her mom? Or do I need to refresh your memory?" *Cough*—"Jail"—*cough*.

Brittany shifted uncomfortably in her seat at the reminder of her humiliation after she'd attacked my mother at the ABLC banquet.

Hannah went in for the kill. "I'd be *ever so happy* to fill Trevor in about it, too. I mean, if he's going to be sticking his tongue down your throat, he's got a right to know where you've been, doesn't he? And I'm sure he'd love to see the photos we took of you being hauled off, which happen to be right here on my cell phone—"

"All right! God, you two are so mean!"

"Speaking of mean, maybe you can return the earrings you took from Morgan," Hannah said.

"Fine." Brittany pulled them out of her earlobes and threw them in my lap.

"Thank you," I said politely. Hannah and I exchanged smiles, and we couldn't help it if they were a tad gleeful.

The orchestra below played a musical flourish. Then the curtain rose and the program began.

Mom and the queen looked awesome together onstage. I sniffed sentimentally at the speeches of friendship and mutual respect. I rose when Mom prompted, and the cheers from the crowd really felt genuine.

The music wasn't half bad, either. I wasn't digging the orchestral rendition of a Beatles medley, but there were a few kicking licks on other Anglo-American tunes that kept the concert from being completely boring.

Afterward, Trevor sidled up to me. I quashed an involuntary shudder. "Hey, Morgan. Would you, ah, be averse to me taking your mate Brittany out for a post-concert nosh?"

"Mind? Why would I mind?"

"Well." He lowered his voice confidentially. "Don't take this personally, love, but it means that I'm moving on. We had a good thing, lots of special memories, but it's over now. *We're* over. Now, now. Don't cry."

I guess he took my strangled snort of laughter for a sob. "It's disappointing, but somehow my heart will go on."

"Cheers, Morgan. Thanks for being brave."

"Best of luck to you both. Oh, and, Trev, make sure you increase the limit on your credit card. Brittany has expensive tastes."

Hannah and I watched with amusement while Brittany snaked her arm around Trevor's waist and headed toward the prime minister's entourage waiting downstairs. Brittany giggled when Trevor squeezed her bum.

"Man, those two are MTB." Hannah shook her head.

"Yeah, a couple of reptiles. But yay for us, because we finally got rid of her."

"Yeah. Tonight we won't have to worry about ditching her. Now we can relax. Maybe Rich will even call."

Hannah's face went all dreamy, like it always did when she thought about Prince Richard. I felt myself go all dreamy, too, because as soon as I could, I was contacting Max. I had to convince him that breaking up with me would be a *big mistake*.

George appeared before me. Grim. So very grim.

"The president is asking for you. And me. And you." She pointed to Hannah. "At the motorcade. Now."

I winced. This wasn't going to be pretty.

Chapter Twenty-four

Once we were all assembled in the unmarked limo and Parker had secured the area, Mom did that thing when she puts the pressure on. She waited.

The silence pulsed in the cab. George handled the anxiety pretty well, but Hannah looked nauseous. It's not easy having the president of the United States glare at you like she's contemplating sending you to a federal penitentiary.

Finally I couldn't take seeing them suffer anymore. "You would have done the same thing if you'd been in my shoes, Mom."

"Really, Morgan? Do you honestly think I would have jeopardized our relationship with our closest ally so I could chitchat about Hannah with the queen of England?"

"How did you know about that?"

"Because Her Majesty mentioned it to me in passing when *I* finally met her."

"Oh." I guess we'd never thought through that part of the plan, though it was obvious in hindsight.

"And you." Mom turned to George and zapped her with a fierce look. "You enabled them."

"Yes." George's pixie face never changed, but her knuckles whitened.

I jumped in. "I forced George into it, Mom—"

"It's all my fault—" Hannah began at the same time.

"I should have stuck to protocol—" George was saying.

Mom held up her hand to stop the three of us from talking over one another. "I don't want to hear excuses from *any* of you." She glared at the three of us. "Hannah, I'd like both you and George to exit the limo. I have a few words I want to say to my daughter. Alone. And if either of you ever speak of this again, you can forget clemency."

George and Hannah couldn't scramble out of the car fast enough.

Now my mother and I sat in stony silence. Well, it was stony on her part. On mine, it was closer to terrified.

She sighed, and all the anger drained out of her. "Morgan, what were you thinking? Do you know how dangerous impersonating me is?"

"I had a good reason."

"You think helping a friend with her love life is enough of a reason? What if you had gotten caught? Or if the queen had no sense of humor regarding her grandson? I had to do some quick thinking when I met her to cover your tracks. You put me in an embarrassing situation with a major head of state, Morgan."

"Oh." I hadn't thought about how my encounter with the queen would impact Mom.

"I wish you would learn to make better decisions," Mom continued. Disappointment suffused her voice. "You're an Abbott, and you need to be more careful about the repercussions of your actions."

Indignation welled up in me. She was right. I wasn't a kid anymore. I knew all about being responsible for my actions. I would take whatever punishment she decided to dish out. I deserved it.

"Maybe I do make screwy decisions sometimes," I said. "But when I make a choice, I usually have a good reason. There are some things, really important things worth risking everything for. Hannah is definitely one of those things. She needed me, and I was the only one who could help her."

Now that I'd gotten started, I was finding it hard to shut up. "I don't need a lecture on how I'm the daughter of the president, and how I need to behave appropriately and conform to expectations—I've been doing that ever since you became president. In fact, my whole life is ruled by what people expect of the president's daughter. I'm getting soooo sick of worrying how disappointed everyone will be if I don't meet those expectations. Including you. I know I can royally screw things up. But I'm trying to live my life the best I can."

"This isn't about Hannah anymore, is it?" Mom asked when I paused for breath.

"I don't think so." Really, it wasn't.

"Go on."

"I don't want to go to any of the colleges that have floated offers for me. They only want me because I'm your daughter."

"Oh, come on, honey—"

"You've seen my report card. My crappy GPA. Heck, you talk to Ms. Gibson on a monthly basis about my lousy grades. It's so obvious that these colleges want *me* because of *you*."

Mom couldn't refute it. "So what do you want?"

I took a deep breath. "I want to go to culinary school and study to become a chef."

"A chef. Interesting."

"I think I'd make a great one," I said. "I love to cook, and I'm really good at it. It's the one thing I know I can excel at. I'd ace my classes in culinary school for sure."

"Anything else?" Mom prodded when I fell silent.

I took a deep breath. "I'm dating Max Jackson."

"Ah" was all Mom said. She gazed at me like she was seeing me for the first time.

I steeled myself for a lecture.

"It's about time you came clean, Morgan. I was wondering when you and Max would figure it out."

"What?"

"Oh, come on, sweetie. Don't you know it's impossible to keep secrets when you're being watched twenty-four-seven in the bubble? And I'm your mother. Don't you think I can see a change in you? I've known about Max since the moment you met each other in the Oval Office. It was pretty clear the two of you were going to be an item."

"You . . . *knew*?"

"Of course. The way you made his life hell the first few weeks on the job confirmed it. I knew you were testing him to see if he was strong enough for you. He seems to be holding up to the workout you're giving him. He's got a good head on his shoulders, and he seems to be the perfect guy for you."

The perfect guy. Except . . .

"It doesn't matter anymore," I said dully. "Max is probably going to get the job with the British SIS division and move to London and date posh British girls with cute accents who don't have National Disaster as a nickname."

"I think Max is smarter than that, Morgan. Give the guy some credit. And trust. In the meantime . . ." Mom flipped open a compartment in the burled wood panel of the limo and pulled out a brochure. "Here."

Le Cordon Bleu. London campus.

"You should follow your dreams no matter where they take you. Even if you are the president's daughter."

I launched into Mom's arms and we hugged each other hard.

Chapter Twenty-five

Parker escorted me back to my unmarked car since Mom would be heading to Buckingham Palace for a long (and guaranteed to be boring) state dinner with the queen. George waited outside the car, her hands folded in the deferential Secret Service stance. Her face, like Max's when he was working as my agent, gave no hint of her feelings. She nodded to Parker for the handoff.

"How'd it go?" she asked as she opened the car door for me.

Agents never opened car doors for their protectees. George was more nervous than she let on.

"Not bad," I told her. "I think we're in the clear."

She let out a breath.

I climbed inside the car and George followed. Hannah was already inside, nibbling on a nail.

"Well?"

I gave her a thumbs-up.

Hannah went limp with relief. "I thought we were in for it. I owe you big time, Morg."

"Nah, don't worry about it. You'd do the same for me if you could."

"You're an awesome friend, ya know?"

"I know." We cracked up and hugged.

"It's still early," I said. "And our last night in London. What do you want to do?"

"To tell you the truth, nothing without Rich. I'm gonna miss him so much."

"I miss Max, too," I said quietly.

It was too harsh being in London without our boyfriends.

"Actually, plans have already been made for you both," George said unexpectedly. "I've been instructed to take you to the London Eye."

"The London Eye? You mean that big Ferris wheel by the Thames River?"

George nodded.

"Wanna go, Hans?"

Hannah shrugged. "Not really. It's seems like the kind of a romantic thing to do with a boyfriend."

"Mom probably thought it'd be a treat for us, but I'm not feeling it, either, George. Why don't you take us back

192

to the hotel?"

George got exasperated. "Come on, girls. Don't let your crappy love lives ruin your last night in London."

"Uh, aren't you supposed to be making us feel better?" I remarked.

"So what if you don't have boyfriends? Go see the sights one last time."

"I guess she's right," Hannah said reluctantly. "It'd be lame not to see at least one major tourist attraction before we leave."

"Fine," I sighed. "We'll go."

We wove through London traffic and crossed the Thames River to the South Bank. The London Eye glowed blue and white against the dusky sky like an enormous wheel of fire. Slowly it churned in a circle. George instructed the driver to swing the car to a cordoned off area right outside the front entrance. A sign on the entrance said THE LONDON EYE IS TEMPORARILY CLOSED TO THE PUBLIC.

Maybe that's why George insisted Hannah and I go, because closing the attraction would be a major hassle and they wouldn't have wanted the effort to go to waste. I supposed Hannah and I would go up on the Eye, take some photos of the London panorama, then be whisked back to the hotel for a night of British comedy on TV and a box of Wall's ice lollies from room service—

"Oh my *god!*" Hannah shrieked. "It's Rich!"

She'd jumped out of the car almost before it came to a full stop. Prince Richard grinned at her from the platform. He looked so hot in a blue pinstripe blazer and a crisp white shirt unbuttoned at the throat.

My own heart leapt. Right next to him stood Max in low-slung jeans and a leather jacket.

I scrambled out after Hannah and headed right into Max's open arms.

"I can't believe you're really here," I said. "I thought you wanted to break up with me."

He pulled back, genuinely shocked. "Where'd you get that idea?"

"Uh, when you said maybe we should take a break?"

"I was trying to give you space," he said. "You know, from all the pressure you're under . . . and . . . stuff . . ."

He trailed off when I started nibbling his earlobe. He was so cute when he got flustered.

"How about I'll tell you when I need space," I said. "Deal?"

"Deal."

"Morgan, guess what?" Hannah yelled from where she was squeezing Prince Richard. "Rich has reserved the entire wheel *just for us*! Isn't that awesome?"

"I thought we needed to celebrate," Richard said with a

cheeky smile that could melt the Eye's steel struts. "Grand-mum decided that she didn't have the right to dictate who I date, and that she trusted my judgment in that respect. I think the president must have said something to her. She's usually not so flexible."

"Oh, *really*?" I winked at Hannah. "That's fantastic news. Mom comes through again."

"I have good news, too," Max said. "I was offered a job with MI6."

"That's so . . . great, Max." I gave him a squeeze, keeping a brave smile on my face. "When do you start?"

"Soon." He brought his head down to mine and murmured, "Disappointed?"

"A little."

"Don't be. I'm assigned to their Washington, D.C., division."

"*Max!*"

This time my hug nearly strangled him. Now that Mom had given me the green light to tell the world about Max, Brittany Whittaker's evil blackmail scheme fell apart. What's more, now that I'd finally come clean to Mom about what I wanted to do with my life, I could start looking at culinary schools once I got home. Everything was starting to fall into place.

We boarded one of the Eye pods and settled in for a

slow ride on the biggest bicycle wheel in the world. The spectacular view of nighttime London took my breath away—as did Max's kisses every couple minutes or so. Richard and Hannah snogged their lips off for most of the ride. I snuggled into Max's arms for the slow revolution over London, and reveled in feeling his heart thumping steadily against my back.

I sighed. Life was just about perfect for the moment.

"Uh-oh," Max said as we headed downward to the landing platform. "Media."

Ugh. Moment over.

A huge gathering of camera crews, paparazzi, and spectators waited below. George and the prince's bodyguards had launched into crowd control. Flashes were already going off and we hadn't even gotten off the Eye pod yet.

I turned to Max. "It's okay if you want to sneak away. I know you're sick of the media zoo."

"I have a better idea."

Max took me firmly by the hand and helped me out of the Eye pod. Camera flashes bathed us in electric light.

"No more secrets," he said. "How about we really steal Brittany's thunder by giving the London paparazzi an exclusive?"

"What sort of exclusive?"

"Let's show them how much I love Morgan Abbott."

"Love?" Was I really hearing this? "You . . . are in love with me?"

"Totally. One hundred percent head over heels in love

with you, Morg. Have been ever since you led me on that goofy chase around the White House."

"Are you sure? I mean, life with me is one disaster after another. Then there's the whole being a celebrity, and the security issues—"

"Morgan?"

"Yeah?"

"You're babbling again."

"I am?"

He walked me to the edge of the Eye platform, in full view of the media and onlookers who had gathered to celebrity stalk. He took my face in his hands and gave me the most awesome kiss of my life. I barely heard the screams from the crowd, I was so in the moment.

When the kiss ended, I heard the crowd gasp again.

Prince Richard had taken Max's lead and was kissing Hannah, too.

And since we were being honest . . .

"Hey, Max," I whispered. "I love you, too."

The smile that lit up his face was brighter than the neon lights radiating from the London Eye. But mine felt even brighter.

Like my future.

★

Cassidy Calloway lives in New Jersey with her fat cat named Kennedy, but she loves visiting Washington, D.C. She wanted to be president of the United States when she grew up but decided to write about it instead. She has a passion for designer shoes and white-chocolate gingersnaps.

★